Missionary Max and the Lost City

Copyright © 2016 Andrew Comings

ISBN-13: 978-1534758902

ISBN-10: 1534758909

Illustrator | Zilson Costa

Publishing and Design Services | MelindaMartin.me

DEDICATION

To Itacyara—aka "The Brazilian Bombshell"—my very own fierce jungle queen, my continuous source of inspiration.

PROLOGUE

Richmond was in flames. It was the third of April, 1865, and Confederate President Jefferson Davis and his cabinet–as well as anybody else with the means–had fled the beleaguered city before the inevitable arrival of General Grant's bluecoats. With nobody left to maintain order, the erstwhile Confederate capital quickly descended into anarchy. Mobs of citizens, escaped prisoners, and ex-slaves roamed the streets in a frenzy of looting and arson.

Through the mayhem a company of smartly dressed Confederate soldiers marched through the streets, westward, away from the rapidly approaching General Grant and his Union hordes. In their midst teams of oxen pulled five large carts, their voluminous contents hidden from view by canvas shrouds. Anyone who cared to look could see from the way the oxen strained at their load that the carts were unusually heavy.

There weren't many who cared to look. A wagon surrounded by soldiers was of no interest to looters when completely unguarded homes and businesses were there for the plundering. So plunder they did, while the greatest treasure in the South rolled unmolested out of the city.

Once safely beyond city limits the cart and its attendants veered south. They continued in a south-by-southeast direction for three days, until finally reaching their destination: a hidden cove on the North Carolina coast. There the contents of the wagon were removed, placed carefully in wooden boats, and rowed to a ship moored nearby. As the guards boarded the ship, they ripped the CSA insignia from their uniforms, revealing underneath a coat of arms featuring a bolt of lightning grasped firmly by a gloved fist. Their leader approached the ship's captain and spoke in Portuguese.

"All is ready, *capitão,*" he reported.

"Excellent work, *tenente. Doutor* Santana will be pleased." With that he gave the order to weigh anchor, and the warship slipped silently out to sea. As she rode the waves, bearing south by southeast, she flew no flag. Yet a full moon illuminated the nameplate on her side. It read *Lua Negra.*

Eighty years later, almost to the day, World War Two was grinding to a close and the Third Reich was gasping its last, tortured breaths. The city of Berlin was a blazing inferno. An increasingly insane Adolf Hitler had holed himself up in a bunker accompanied by his mistress and his most sycophantic followers, while the city descended into a fiery chaos outside.

Between charred buildings and over pockmarked roads, two military trucks wound through the darkened city. They were preceded by an armored car. Another followed close behind. German soldiers stood ready at the gun turrets and rode as passengers, their Mausers primed and at the ready. Once outside they picked up speed, heading northwest, bouncing over country roads.

As the morning light began to crack over the war-torn horizon, the vehicles pulled into a hidden cove near the coastal city of Bremerhaven. In the murky water could be seen the black outlines of two U-boats. All the soldiers left the trucks and armored cars and began to unload the contents.

It was hard work; removing heavy boxes–in particular one rather strange-looking box that resembled an oversized coffin–putting them in small rowboats, and loading them to the waiting U-boats. But the men worked with typical German efficiency, and before the sun had fully risen both submarines slipped below the surface, taking with them the officers and all the contents of the trucks.

Once under the frigid waters of the North Atlantic the captain of the first boat turned from peering through his periscope to the officer beside him. Unlike those of the rest of the crew, their uniforms no longer bore German insignia. In its place, there was a bolt of lightning gripped by a gloved fist.

"It should take us about three days," he said in German. "Then we will arrive at Cabrito. *Herr* Santana will be very pleased."

April 3, 1985. The twin-prop passenger plane bucked and wheeled, buffeted by the winds of a tropical depression over the Atlantic, en-route from Kingston, Jamaica to Santo Expedito–capital city of the little island nation called Cabrito. The plaintive whine of its laboring engines was accompanied by the howling wind. Inside, the terrified passengers huddled in their seats and prayed fervently to their respective deities. Towards the back of the plane, Tina Swansen clutched her infant daughter, Amanda, to her chest while Scott, her husband, made every effort to reassure her.

"It's going to be okay, hon."

The Swansens were on their way from the US to the Cabritan islands as missionaries–the first Protestant missionaries to attempt a ministry on the small, mid-Atlantic republic in almost a decade.

In the cockpit the pilots had come to the horrifying conclusion that their little craft was not going to weather the storm. Desperately, they fought with the controls, trying with all their might to bring the plane down for a water landing. Just when they thought they might be making some progress, the lights flickered once, twice, and then went out. The pilots removed their hands from the useless controls and looked at each other in desperation.

Back in the darkened cabin, Scott Swansen hugged his wife, and Tina hugged her baby.

"Please God," she whispered with all her motherly instinct, "save my little girl!"

Four shadowy figures stood under the palms, sheltered from the rain that lashed their island home. The ever-nearing sound they heard–different from the howl of the storm–caused them to look up. They saw an object pass over them at a tremendous speed. Most certainly it was one of the god-bearers that they saw arrive at the distant island three times a day. Yet this one was lower, and not headed in the usual direction.

They watched, amazed, as it hit the ocean about 200 yards from where they stood, sending spray in all directions. Through the lightning flashes they saw that the god-bearer had broken open, and within a matter of minutes it had slipped beneath the waves.

In the diminishing rainfall the dark-skinned observers made their way to the water's edge, their eyes straining in the darkness for any clue as to the meaning of this strange omen. As they were about to turn and leave, the clouds suddenly parted and the moon reflected brightly on the ocean. And there, in the middle of the moonbeam, a small baby floated towards them on a red cushion. It was crying softly.

Four sets of arms reached out to pull the baby in. Strong, gentle hands lifted it from the cushion and examined it from head to toe, picking at the strange pink clothes, and gingerly fingering the heart-shaped locket around its neck. They had no idea that the strange script engraved on the front read "Amanda," or that, if they opened it, they would see a picture of Scott and Tina Swansen, holding the same little girl they now held in their arms.

And as they ran through the jungle carrying the present the great Tan had given them, the remains of the passenger plane sunk deeper and deeper into the murky waters, until they came to rest on the ocean floor mere meters from the sunken hulk of a German U-boat.

CHAPTER 1

REUNITED, AND IT FEELS SO...STRANGE

Maxwell Sherman, known as "Missionary Max" to an increasing number of the residents of the island of Cabrito, felt as if he were facing his execution. He was fairly certain that this was not how one was supposed to feel while standing in the airport awaiting the arrival of one's girlfriend, and yet there was no denying it–that was exactly how he felt.

"You must be so excited to see her after all this time." The observation came from the raven-haired girl standing next to him. "What has it been... six months?" Ilana, the beautiful native woman he had met in the marketplace (and then saved from a horde of angry tribesmen intent on turning them both into human shish kebab) looked at him with an innocent grin, her eyes dancing. "I so want to meet her. She must be a special girl to have captured the heart of the great Missionary Max."

"Yes, she's very special." Max agreed, although not with much conviction. He was wondering what Mary Sue's reaction to the presence of Ilana would be.

Ilana had insisted on coming, and Raymond Sand, the gruff American jack-of-all trades, had insisted on bringing them in his rattletrap Volkswagen Beetle that served as a part-time taxi. As Ray had been instrumental in getting them out of a rather close scrape with death in the dense Cabritan jungle, Max didn't feel comfortable turning him down. Not to mention the fact that Ray was Ilana's father–something she had discovered shortly after their dramatic evacuation from the rainforest.

Max, who had faced down jihadists, drug runners, and most recently, a horde of maddened tribal warriors without losing his nerve, felt a tremendous sense of anxiety as he awaited Mary Sue's flight. He had grown to love the island of Cabrito in the short time he had lived there. He loved its people, its many cultures blended into one, its lively music, its colorful dress, its delicious (if different) food–and he was not at all sure how Mary Sue would react to these things.

Igreja da Paz–Peace Church, the little congregation where Max had become the reluctant pastor upon the hasty exit of the original missionaries, was doing much better than Max could have anticipated. The incident on the runway back in October had caused a few of the soldiers present to come to services out of sheer curiosity. Some had returned with their families, and Max was having weekly Bible studies with three of them.

Max was getting a few hundred dollars a month in support from his home church in Upstate New York. He supplemented this meager income by giving martial-arts lessons. His reputation in this area had grown after word spread of his performance at the Yamani festival. There he had defeated–in friendly hand-to-hand combat–the best of the Yamani warriors. Then he had bested millionaire *empresario*–and the island's de-facto ruler–Emídio Santana, who had actually been trying to kill him.

The income from the American church and the martial arts lessons allowed him to rent a little apartment in the Cidade Antiga, the old colonial section of Santo Expedito–little changed since its establishment by the Portuguese almost five centuries earlier. Looking out his iron-latticed apartment window, Max could imagine the Portuguese colonists, in their 16th and 17th century finery, walking the same narrow cobblestone streets, greeting friends and neighbors and plying their wares.

It was a beautiful setting, yet, try as he might, he could not picture Mary Sue thriving there. Life in Cabrito was raw and unvarnished, and Max knew that Mary Sue Perkins was accustomed to "well-cooked and varnished."

Not that there was anything particularly wrong with that. Max had to admit that this was actually one of the things that had attracted Max to her in the first place. She was innocently naive, blissfully unaware of the evil in the world—a subject with which Max, a former Green Beret whose résumé included special operations in many parts of the world, was all too familiar.

In the sheltered Perkins home Max had found a stable, loving family atmosphere, which, if a little stifling at times, was something he desperately longed for. He had not known the safety of a healthy family relationship since his father died when he was a teenager. When he met Mary Sue and her family, he had found it again.

No doubt about it, Mary Sue was beautiful, proper, and...safe.

Then there was Ilana. The island girl, raised in the jungle and educated at Columbia University, was anything but "safe." In fact, she could be straight up dangerous. On the day of their first encounter Max had watched her flip a would-be mugger onto his back. Then he had accompanied her to a banquet at the presidential mansion where she seemed perfectly at ease among the high society of Cabrito. A few days later he saw her in her ceremonial native garb (and paint, lots of paint) leading the feverish festival dances of the Yamani people. And that very night they ran for their lives through the jungle, chased by a horde of Yamani warriors bent on turning them both into human pincushions.

No, safe she was not. But she was full of life! Her emotions ran deep and full. Her dark eyes could be pools of sadness one minute, and sparkle with merriment the next. Her laughter was infectious, her energy knew no bounds. And in the months since his arrival on Cabrito, Max had found himself increasingly drawn to her.

Max shook his head. *This will never do...* The sound of propellers mercifully interrupted his thoughts.

Through the second-floor observation window he saw the twin-prop plane drop its landing gear, touch down rather haphazardly, and then slow to a stop on the runway. The aluminum stairway was rolled into place and before long passengers began to disembark.

"Look! There she is! I recognize her from the pictures," Ilana squealed excitedly. Max squinted to make out the passengers through the streaked window pane. The girl descending the staircase had flowing blond hair and was wearing a blue-jean jumper that went all the way to her feet.

As he watched his Mary Sue he reflected on how Ilana, the unwitting source of his inner conflict, was much more excited to see his girlfriend than he was.

If she only knew...

Ilana tugged impatiently at his sleeve. "C'mon Max! She's almost here!"

Max and Ilana went down the stairs and over to the "foreign arrivals" door. In a surreal sort of way it occurred to Max that all arrivals at the Santo Expedito International Airport were foreign, as there was no other airport on the small archipelago in the middle of the Atlantic.

"Maaaaaaaax!"

The voice was Mary Sue's. He looked up to see her running across the lobby to meet him. In an instant she was in his arms. As Max held her, the doubts that had assailed his mind began to melt away. Her closeness, her familiar perfume... he squeezed her tight, and then looked into her upturned face. Those big, innocent blue eyes, the pert little nose, the ruby-red lips... Max instinctively bent in to kiss her.

"No no! You know better, Maxwell Sherman. The first kiss is for the wedding, remember?" Max remembered, as the climate that had built up came crashing down around him. Mary Sue and Max disengaged and Max turned to Ilana, who was looking at them, her head tilted, quizzically. Max wondered if she had heard that little exchange.

"Mary Sue, I want you to meet my friend Ilana." he said, somewhat awkwardly.

The American girl turned her attention to Ilana. Max noticed a flicker of disapproval on Mary Sue's face as her eyes quickly scanned the island girl's t-shirt and blue-jeans. Mary Sue *never* wore anything but dresses. But then she smiled and extended her hand.

"Heeeeloooooooo" she said slowly, exaggerating every vowel that came out of her mouth. "Myyyyyy naaaaaame iiiiiiis Maaaary Suuuuuuuue."

Ilana looked surprised, Max's face turned beet red. "Er... Mary Sue, Ilana speaks perfect English. She studied at Columbia University."

Ilana quickly recovered her composure and took Mary Sue's hand. "It's a pleasure to meet you, Mary Sue," she said, with the characteristic twinkle in her eye. "Max has told me a lot about you."

"Oh, yes. Well, it's good to meet you too." An awkward silence followed. Finally Ilana spoke up.

"So, no kiss until the wedding day, huh?" So she *had* heard it.

"Yes," replied Mary Sue. "Max and I decided that would be the best, most God-honoring thing to do. Isn't that right, Maxie Pie?"

Ilana arched her eyebrow. "Maxie Pie?"

"It's my pet name for him. And he calls me 'Suzie Poo', don't you, Maxie Pie?"

Max blushed to the very core of his being. His input into the kissing moratorium had been minimal, he had had absolutely no part in choosing the pet name "Suzie Poo," much less "Maxie Pie."

"No kissing until the wedding." Ilana mused. "Well, I think that's so... romantic."

"You do?" Max asked, incredulously.

A mischievous grin spread across her face. "Sure, Maxie Pie."

Once again Max's face became redder than his hair. "So, Mary Sue, you must have some luggage?" He suggested, desperately trying to change the subject.

"Yes! Yes I do."

"The baggage claim is this way," said Ilana. "You two lovebirds follow me."

Minutes later they were all standing next to the baggage claim belt, looking at the six jumbo suitcases Mary Sue had brought.

What can she possibly have in all those suitcases? Max wondered.

"I would have brought more," Mary Sue said, as if reading his thoughts, "but I'm only staying for two weeks, so I just packed the essentials."

Max and Ilana both looked at her, and it dawned on them that she was completely serious. Finally Max spoke.

"Um… we may have a problem getting all this into Ray's taxi."

"My Dad has an airplane!" suggested Ilana with a grin. Max shot her a withering glance.

"Well, no sense waiting around." Max said, reaching out and grabbing the handles of two suitcases. Ilana did the same, and they began rolling the enormous volumes toward the door. Looking back, Max saw that Mary Sue was just standing there, looking at the remaining two bags. "Are you coming?" he asked.

"Isn't there someone we can pay, like a coolie or something, to carry these two bags?"

"That's India, and no, the taxi's right outside the door," Max explained, a little exasperation creeping into his voice.

"In that case, I'll just wait here while you take those cases, then you can come back for the rest." Ilana glanced at Max, who just rolled his eyes. Ilana shrugged and they both began wheeling the suitcases to the door.

Ray was leaning on the yellow Volkswagen beetle that served as his taxi when the two arrived. His eyes widened at the size of the suitcases.

"No she's not moving here." Max answered Ray's unasked question. "And there are two more where these came from."

Ray let out a low whistle. "Shoulda brought the plane."

"That's what I told Maxie Pie here," said Ilana brightly.

Ray's eyebrow arched in the same way his daughter's had moments earlier. Max shook his head and turned to get the rest of

Mary Sue's baggage, muttering under his breath about apples and trees and the relative falling distance of the former from the latter.

On the other side of Santo Expedito, in the presidential mansion that the residents of Cabrito called the *casa branca, Presidente* Osvaldo Ferraz was smoldering with resentment. The catalyst of his ire was the way Emídio Santana–scion of the wealthy Santana family and *de facto* kingmaker on Cabrito–waltzed in and out of the executive palace like he owned the place. Only the fact that he owed his title, his position, his power–probably even his life–to Dr. Santana kept him from blowing up every time it happened.

Overgrown rich kid! Ferraz muttered under his breath. *Daddy's away, and the big boy must play.*

Emídio Santana, son of billionaire financier George Santana, sat casually behind the desk (*my desk,* Ferraz reflected bitterly), feet propped up on its mahogany surface. Behind him, to the right, stood the woman known to Ferraz only as Conchita. She was dressed in a black business suit that perfectly combined her jet-black hair and man-with-no-eyes sunglasses. And all of these matched the shiny black of the Berretta 92 holstered at her waist. A *beret*, also black, completed the ensemble. It bore an insignia on the flash: a lightning bolt behind a shield.

The insignia was a new addition, one that had caused the *presidente* brief pause when he had first noticed it a few weeks past. It wasn't used by the Cabritan military, that much he knew. Something in the back of his head had clicked, as if he had seen the "lightning shield" before, but with everything else going on there was little time to think about an odd military patch. Indeed, what bothered him more than the patch was the woman who was wearing it.

Ever since the debacle on the runway of the Santo Expedito airport, which had seriously damaged Emídio Santana's standing in the military, he had taken to traveling with Conchita at his side.

And even though Conchita had been taken out of commission rather quickly by a blow to the back of the head on that fateful day, it was clear she was, under normal circumstances, not someone to be trifled with.

President Ferraz had a reputation on Cabrito for being a prodigious ladies' man, and he had tried to work his flirtatious magic on Conchita the first time they had met. The response was an unchanging, stony glare. It was the same expression she wore on her face right now, and it annoyed him to no end.

"I trust my plans meet with official presidential approval." Emídio was talking. "This is an important step for the security of our little republic."

"Let me see if I understand," replied the *presidente*. "We are creating a special force of elite, highly trained warriors, under your direct command. Is that right?"

"Exactly!" Santana smiled.

"And the reason, again?"

"The reason is that the performance of the regular army has been, shall we say, unsatisfactory, of late. I worry for the safety of my beloved island home."

The reason, thought Ferraz, *is that you were thoroughly humiliated by an old woman in front of the army and they will no longer do your bidding, so you need to find other people to carry out your dirty work.* Wisely, he left this thought unsaid.

"Now, we won't need to train these soldiers, because they will come to us already trained," Emídio explained.

"And where on Cabrito are you going to find men with the kind of training you are talking about? I only know of one, and I doubt very much that he would be willing join your little...squad."

Santana's brow furrowed at this obvious reference to the *gringo* people were beginning to refer to as Missionary Max. Was Ferraz needling him? Of all the impertinence! He would have to be dealt with later.

"If you are referring to that insufferable American, rest assured, the last chapter of that story has not been written. Nobody makes a mockery of Emídio Santana and lives to tell about it." Santana looked at Ferraz and repeated, pointedly, "Nobody."

Ferraz swallowed hard. "So, I have the honor of your presence and of the ever-lovely Conchita (He glanced to see if his compliment had had any effect. It hadn't.) because..."

"Because of course I want to do everything legally, and we need your signature on this authorization."

Ferraz almost choked at the word "legally." There had been no such concern when Santana mounted a huge narcotics-producing operation in the jungle, using Cabritan military resources for its protection.

No, the reason for this sudden concern for legality was obvious. *He wants a scapegoat,* he reflected ruefully. *If something goes wrong, it will be my name on the document, not his. He will have plausible deniability, and I'll take the hit.*

Still, Ferraz removed a pen from his shirt pocket and bent over the desk (*his* desk, blast it!) to sign the paper that Santana slid towards him.

"Just one thing..." Ferraz looked up from the desk, pen poised over the paper.

"What is it?" Santana was impatient.

"This elite force we are bringing in...for our own protection of course...what is it called?"

"*Força Relâmpago*...the Lightning Force."

Ferraz' eyes flicked to the insignia on Conhita's beret, and in an instant he knew what was happening. If he signed that paper, any advantage he had as Commander-in-Chief of the Cabritan armed forces–such as they were–would be negated by the presence of a highly trained army that answered only to Santana.

But, having no other option, he bent over the desk and signed the document.

Santana beamed at him. "Very good, *senhor presidente.* You can rest assured that you have made the right decision for the security of our beloved nation. Together with the emergency measures to be carried out shortly, this will guarantee the stability of your administration for the foreseeable future. Do you understand what I'm saying?"

Osvaldo Ferraz understood perfectly. His was a game of survival, and for the present his survival depended on his cooperation with the Santana family. Of that he was certain.

Still, at this juncture, it wouldn't hurt to have a little insurance…

And as Santana and Conchita left his office President Ferraz sat down at his desk (finally!) and racked his brain to think of what that insurance might be.

Back at the airport, Max, Ray, and Ilana were tying Mary Sue's massive suitcases to the roof while Mary Sue watched. With a final tug on the chord, Ray turned to Max and wiped his brow. "There, I think that will hold." he said. "Let's go. Ilana and Mary Sue, you can ride in back. Maxie Pie can ride up front with me."

Max rolled his eyes, knowing that he would probably never live the name down.

"Finally!" exclaimed Mary Sue as Max held the door open for her to get in the rattletrap Volkswagen. "Such a long wait… and after a *very* uncomfortable flight."

As Max closed the door and walked around to the other side, he reflected on his own first ride in the rusty beetle, and shook his head. *Mary Sue, you haven't seen anything yet.*

As the sun began to set over the ocean, a thin man in military fatigues picked his way over rocks and driftwood on a narrow strip of beach that accompanied the edge of the *Ipuna* jungle. His eyes scanned the thick vegetation until at last they found a large embankment. A narrow, almost unnoticeable trail wound up through the tall grass and into the trees where they grew densely together. The man followed it until he came to another embankment. A crude cave had been dug into its face, and smoke rose up lazily from a small fire. A second man sat in front of the fire, as fat as the first man was thin.

"Did you find it?" The fat man's question was in the tongue of the Yamani tribe.

"I did… It was right where you said it would be." Diego held up an object carefully wrapped in a bright red cloth.

"Give it to me."

"First, you must know that it was not easy convincing the great Santana of the truth of your story. He was less than impressed with your service six moons ago."

"Bah." Owanalehe spat into the fire, causing it to sizzle and spark. "How was I to know that the flying machine would appear? If it weren't for that crazy old man, both Missionary Max and that girl would be dead." He rubbed his ample stomach wistfully.

"Nevertheless," continued Diego, "Santana became interested when I mentioned your tale of Emerald Island. He has named you chief of all the tribes to be found there, with me…" here Diego cleared his throat, "with me as the official coordinator of Yamani affairs."

Owanalehe stared at the thin soldier through beady eyes. His partnership with this devious, wheedling little man was one of convenience, nothing more. Both were hungry for power, and, for the time being, they could help each other obtain it. The cunning Yamani witch doctor knew, however, that this would only be a temporary alliance–and an inconvenient one at that.

"Very well," he said at last. "Did the great and generous Santana say anything else?"

"As a matter of fact, he did." Diego shifted on both feet, not certain how the old Indian would accept what he was about to say. "The great and, as you say, generous Santana has ordered a troop of skilled warriors to the Emerald Island to insure our success."

Owanalehe grunted. This was not at all to his liking, but he saw nothing he could do about it. He would have to put up with the intruders until he had taken his revenge, then he could deal with them in their turn. But in order for him to get the vengeance he so desperately wanted, he needed the object in Diego's hand.

"The great and generous Santana is also very wise," he intoned, solemnly. "Now, if you please…" he held out his hand. Somewhat reluctantly, Diego handed him the object.. Owanalehe slowly pulled back the folds, then triumphantly held up its contents: a gold necklace from which hung a green pendant in the shape of a leering monkey. Diego couldn't help but notice that the expression on the face of Owanalehe was almost identical to that of the emerald primate.

CHAPTER 2

MAIDEN THE USA

Though living on Cabrito had never been part of his plan, now that he had been there for six months, Maxwell Sherman could not fathom the thought of leaving. From the time he woke up in the morning to the time he went to bed at night, life on the tropical island offered nonstop adventure and discovery. He thrilled at finding yet another back street, trying another culinary novelty (usually at the home of his friend Bernardinho) or finding some forgotten relic of this island's storied past.

And yet, with all of this, if there was a time he looked forward to most every week, it was the Sunday evening worship with his little congregation. He eagerly anticipated every aspect of the service. The Cabritan people were naturally musical, and the song service was beautiful and heartfelt. Most of the hymns they sang were American or European in origin, but the congregation gave them an island flavor their composers never dreamed of.

But the part Max enjoyed most was the sermon. This had surprised him at first, given how he had initially reacted to the prospect of preaching with anxiety bordering on sheer terror. But now, a few short months later, there was nothing that thrilled him more than the privilege of standing in front of that group of people and sharing what he had learned from the Bible. He had chuckled more than once at the notion of his professors from his brief stint in college seeing him now, pouring over the Bible and other reference works, making sure he got everything right before presenting it to the congregation. They would certainly find no similarity between this Max and the party-boy Max who rarely cracked open a text book during his short but colorful career in higher education.

For their part, the Cabritan congregation loved their new, unintentional missionary, green though he was. He brought a freshness and enthusiasm to the Bible that they had never seen before. And, discontent with mere platitudes, he consistently strove to draw out the meaning of the Scripture text he was expounding. They tolerated—and even looked forward to—his occasional trip-ups in the Portuguese/Creole language of the island.

And indeed, this of itself was a novelty. While previous missionaries had spoken in pure Portuguese (considered the language of the elite on Cabrito) *Missionário* Max made every effort to speak in the hybrid language spoken by most of the people in their everyday lives. This endeared him all the more to his congregation.

There had been some raised eyebrows at first, and even a couple accusations of "profaning" the holy text. But Max did his homework, and was careful to explain that since the founding of the Church, the word of God had been presented in the common language of the people—beginning with the New Testament texts that were written in the language of the grocery lists and sales receipts of ancient Greece. For this and many other pieces of information he was grateful for the small library left behind by the Blakes in their hurry to flee Cabrito.

Thinking of the Blakes caused Max's mind to wander briefly in a different direction. He had heard nothing from the missionary family that were his predecessors since that day in the airport—his first in Crabrito, and their last. At times he was tempted to question their decision to leave Cabrito, but Santana had threatened their young sons, and Max knew that many men who face adversity unflinchingly will crumble at the prospect of any harm coming to their children.

Whatever the case, that fateful moment in the airport had changed Max's life forever. Instead of returning to the US after two weeks with pictures for a scrapbook and little else, Max had found himself plunged into the intrigue and adventure of life on Cabrito, and his heart intertwined with the life of the little Peace Church.

Perhaps most surprisingly of all to Max, the little church was growing. Besides the soldiers and their families, several people from the surrounding communities, as well as some of Max's neighbors from the Old City had begun to attend. Some were merely curious to see what this *gringo* called Missionary Max was all about. Others, however, were clearly being transformed by the Gospel.

The service was almost over. Max had preached his heart out from one of his favorite parts of Genesis–the account of Abraham, his almost-sacrifice of Isaac, and God's last minute provision of a ram. The story had "Jesus" written all over it, and it was that kind of thing that Max enjoyed preaching the most.

Now he was standing off to the side as three teens led the congregation in a final hymn. His eyes scanned the school-room the congregation had been using since their chapel had burnt down shortly after Max's arrival in Cabrito. During the week around fifty children of varying ages and one harried teacher used this space. The wooden desks were currently piled up to one side making room for several rows of plastic chairs, divided by an aisle down the middle. From the ceramic-tiled ceiling a single fan whirred and vibrated in a valiant-yet-futile effort to keep the air circulating.

Yes, it was a far cry from the picturesque, Civil War-era sanctuary where he had worshiped back in Upstate New York, yet Max had never felt himself to be more a part of the Body of Christ than he did here. His heart was full as he contemplated each person in attendance. Bernardinho–his first real Cabritan friend–was there with his family. His daughter Isabela–Max's translator back in the days when he needed one–was one of the teens leading the singing. A few benches back sat Ray. He was still "on the fence with the whole religion thing" (his words), but he came every Sunday with his daughter Ilana, and seemed to pay attention.

Ilana herself was growing in her faith by leaps and bounds. Since finding Jesus that day in the jungle, surrounded by angry Yamani Indians intent on making a meal of them both, she had taken to her new faith with a passion. Almost daily she telephoned Max with questions about the meaning of one Bible passage or another.

Now, during the service, as Max continued to scan the little congregation, his eyes rested on Mary Sue. She was conspicuous, and it was not just because of her pale skin, blond hair and blue eyes. While the Cabritans–a naturally close people with little notion of "personal space"–sat shoulder to shoulder on the long wooden benches, the American girl sat several inches away from the nearest person. Back when they were both in the U.S. her parents had enforced a "six inch rule" on them, indicating how close they could be to each other at any given time. By the looks of it, Mary Sue had taken that rule to heart and expanded it to a whole foot.

Ten days with Mary Sue in Cabrito had been tense, to say the least. A more accurate word might be "excruciating." She reacted adversely to just about everything she saw. The sights, sounds, and smells of the open-air market frightened and disgusted her. The food made her sick. Her living quarters–a spare room at Bernardinho's house–though comfortable by Cabritan standards, was nothing compared to her pillow-filled quarters back home.

In fact, to Max's great annoyance, she had begun to compare everything she saw to America–out loud. He had lost count of how many times she had begun a sentence with the words "In the United States we…"

Even more annoying was her attitude towards Ilana. It was obvious that Mary Sue was threatened by the beautiful girl from the jungle, and she took every opportunity to belittle her in Max's eyes.

"Are you sure she's a Christian, Max? I saw her wearing shorts."

"I read that the jungle people here are cannibals. Wouldn't it be weird if you found out Ilana has actually eaten people?"

"It would be great if Ilana could spend some time in America so she could see how real Christian girls act."

This last declaration was made to Max, in Ilana's presence. Ilana, who had endured Mary Sue's asides up until that point with magnificent aplomb, was visibly taken aback. She turned abruptly and walked away. Mary Sue sighed.

"Some people just can't handle the truth."

Max had put up with Mary Sue's attitude so far, but seeing the effect her acid tongue had on Ilana, he could no longer be quiet.

"Listen, Mary Sue, I don't know what you expected to find when you came here, but you need to understand that this isn't the farm country of Upstate New York. You can't expect the people here to act like Americans, because they aren't. They are Cabritans, and there are a lot of things that they do that Americans could learn from. And," here he took a deep breath, "there are a lot of things that you could learn from Ilana."

Saying that made Max feel good–at least for the moment. Mary Sue, on the other hand, was mortified. Back before Max had started this wild (and somewhat ill-advised, she could see now) escapade in Cabrito he had always deferred to her spiritual maturity. She wasn't sure what had happened to "her Maxie-pie," but she most certainly didn't like it.

"What could I possibly learn from her?" she asked, incredulously. "She, she...." Max interrupted her before she could finish.

"She knows how to hold her tongue," he said, and immediately he regretted his inability to do the same. Mary Sue's eyes watered up, her lips trembled, and, with a stomp of her foot, she turned and ran into Bernadinho's home and to her room. She didn't appear for the rest of the day, not even when Bernadinho's wife called her down for supper.

Later Ray had asked him if everything was alright. He said Ilana was very upset, wondering what she had done to offend Mary Sue.

"Max, I don't claim to know much about the womenfolk," he had said in his typical, straightforward manner, "but it seems to me that this here girlfriend of yours needs an attitude adjustment."

That dramatic episode had taken place Saturday morning. Now it was Sunday night, and as he stood before the congregation waiting for the last notes of the final hymn to die down, he noticed that

Mary Sue's eyes were still somewhat red. She had been glaring at him during the entire service.

Then the back door of the auditorium opened, and with amazing swiftness his upset girlfriend became the least of Max's worries.

CHAPTER 3

FIRE, OR DYING EMBERS?

ix Yamani warriors–spears held firmly in their hands, faces painted for war–marched silently, single file, into the auditorium and stood at attention behind the back row of chairs. The three young people leading the singing and the man accompanying on guitar noticed them at the same time Max did, and the last line of the hymn trailed off and died in their mouths. The congregation, wondering what was going on, craned their necks around to see what Max and the song leaders were seeing. When they saw the warriors, gasps and a couple muffled screams escaped from the audience. Mary Sue turned several shades paler–something many in the congregation would have believed impossible up until that moment.

His mind racing into overdrive, Max caught Ilana's eye and motioned with his head to the back of the auditorium. She nodded, then she stood up to approach the warriors. Out of the corner of his eye Max saw that Ray had moved to stand casually off to the side. Max knew his friend was packing, and that he was subtly positioning himself for a clean shot should things get out of hand.

While Max appreciated Ray's gesture, he *really* hoped things didn't go that far. If there were any kind of panic on the part of the congregation, the scene had the potential to get very ugly, very quickly.

With that in mind, Max stepped to the microphone and spoke to the congregation. "*Irmãos,*" he began in Portuguese, "*no ya se corre-corre,*" he finished the phrase in Creole–*don't be frightened.* "This is a group of Yamani from Ilana's tribe, and she is going to talk to them. Don't make any sudden moves. I'm sure there is a perfectly good explanation for why they are here."

He chose not to mention how his last encounter with the Yamani had been on somewhat less-than-cordial terms. Indeed, among the men standing there, he was sure he recognized some of those who had chased Ilana and himself through the jungle a few short months earlier.

Ilana made her way swiftly to the back, and was soon in animated conversation with the warriors. She was no longer director of FUNAPI, the government agency that dealt with Indian affairs, and the last time she had seen any of them, she had been fleeing from them by Max's side; still, she was one of them and was by far the best equipped to deal directly with the men. Max held his breath, looking for any sign of reaction–positive or negative–in the painted faces of the tribesmen.

It was with great relief that Max saw her embrace one of the men, then another and another until she had hugged the entire group. He felt fairly certain this was a good sign. Ilana looked back at him and signaled that all was well. Max dismissed the congregation, and they exited the building with astonishing rapidity, giving their jungle visitors a wide berth.

Quickly he made his way back to where Ilana was still talking to the natives. He noticed that Ray had come up silently beside him.

"Max!" Mary Sue hissed at him. He paused and turned towards her. "What if it's a trap?"

Max looked at her incredulously.

"I'm serious!" she continued. "What if that Indian girl called them here to... to kill us?"

Ray had come up alongside Max, and shook his head in amazement. "Is she for real?"

Max just rolled his eyes and continued to the back of the auditorium. Ilana met him there.

"Max, these are representatives from all three clans of the Yamani people, and they have come for our help."

"That's a radical change in attitude from the last time we met," Max observed. Ilana couldn't help smiling.

"They say that after we were pulled from the jungle–thanks, Dad–they concluded that there must be a powerful spirit working on our behalf."

"There is."

"A powerful spirit, or an old guy who happened to have an airplane stored in the barn behind his house," muttered Ray, ever the cynic.

After a quick conference they decided that the best place to meet would be Ray's house. The old Portuguese plantation had plenty of space for everybody, and from there it would be easy for the Yamani warriors to slip back into the jungle. Ray left in his old, beat up VW Beetle, and then returned, this time with an equally old, equally beat up VW van. Everybody squeezed inside, including Mary Sue, who at the last minute decided that she'd better go along to keep an eye on things. She insisted, however, on sitting in the passenger seat (much to Ray's chagrin), which left Max and Ilana squeezed in the back with the warriors.

That night, around the fire Ray had hastily built in the back yard, Max listened as the Yamani explained the reason for their presence.

When the Yamani people came across the great sea, we inhabited the green island, the ones you white men call "Esmeralda." It was considered sacred, and there we built a great city called Icxi Xahn. It was a beautiful city, crowned with a glorious temple. From Icxi Xahn the great kings ruled our four great peoples: the Tree People, the Rock People, the Earth People, and the River People. Our nation spread over all the islands that the white men have called 'Cabrito'."

But our ancestors displeased the gods, and great disease fell upon the city dwellers. Such was the death visited upon the island that our people left, and the city was accursed.

Having no ruler, the clans began to fight amongst themselves. After countless years of warfare our brothers the River People tired of the conflict. One day they left, saying they would return to the Green Island, and to Icxi Xahn. The other tribes begged them not to go, but they insisted. They packed their families and belongings in their canoes and rowed out into the ocean, towards the Emerald Island. A great mist came down and covered them, and they were never seen again.

Many times over the years brave Yamani warriors have gone to the Emerald Island to try to find our brothers and let them know that peace has come to us. Often they do not return. Those who do return report seeing warriors like shadows in the trees. Thus we no longer call them "River People" but "Shadow People."

Life continued this way, year after year, century after century, until last week, when suddenly strange warriors burst upon our villages with no warning, killing many men, and taking many prisoners, and then disappearing again into the jungle. Some of our own brave warriors gave chase, and followed them to the ocean, where the invaders boarded canoes and struck out in the direction of the Green Island. Our warriors feared to follow.

And now there is great distress among our people. We do not know why our brothers, the River People, have emerged from the shadows after so long, only to make war on us. Some in our camp want to make war on them in return. Others are afraid, saying that the Shadow People are half man, half spirit. There is a great crying among our people for our brethren who were killed or taken captive.

And so, in a great council, it was remembered how our princess Ilanawehe and her pale friend were snatched from the sky just before we, in our frenzy, were to run them through with our spears. We have been sent as representatives to beseech you to forgive us of our past grievance, and help us in this present trouble.

Max was spellbound by the story. The Yamani had fascinated him since his first night among them, and now he was getting a new window on their history. He wondered how many people at

FUNAPI had such knowledge of the "indigenous people" it was their job to protect. Most likely they were completely unaware of these recent developments.

"I do have one question," said Max. "Whatever became of the rather large witch doctor who got the people whipped up in a frenzy that night in the forest?"

Ilana turned to the warriors. "*Do na Owanalehe?*" she repeated in the Yamani tongue. A look of sadness mixed with consternation came over their faces. They responded, and Ilana translated their answer.

"Apparently he was greatly displeased at our escape. After the warriors returned and told him what happened, he became very agitated, and berated them severely. His harsh words deeply offended many of the warriors. His standing among the people diminished. Then one day, he simply disappeared. They searched for him for several days, but he could not be found." Ilana paused while another warrior interjected something, then continued. "There are rumors spreading through the jungle that he was present when the Shadow People attacked, and that around his neck he wears the Green Monkey."

At the name of his favorite watering hole, Ray's head snapped up. "The Green Monkey? What does a tavern down by the docks have to do with anything?"

"Not the tavern, Dad. It's a monkey's head, carved out of emerald or some green rock. It came into the possession of the tribe many years ago–some say it was even a gift from the gods–and the Yamani revere it. It was passed down from generation to generation of Yamani medicine men, until it was lost in a battle with the white men many years ago.

"The Yamani believe that the man who has The Green Monkey possesses superhuman powers. They also believe it gives them protection, and ascribe any current misfortunes to the fact that is was lost."

"But it's just a trinket!" The exclamation came from Mary Sue, sitting in the corner.

"To us, yes," Max interjected, trying not to let his impatience show. "But jungle cultures like the Yamani are very close to the spirit world, and this kind of thing is very real to them."

Mary Sue gave a response somewhere between a grunt and a snort, and resumed her pout.

One of the warriors spoke again. His words caused some discussion among his friends. Ilana translated: "He says that some villagers claim they saw a woman among the attackers–a woman whose head was on fire. Others say this is ridiculous."

"Hair on fire...like mine?" he ran his hand through his own perennially unruly shock of red hair. Ilana translated, and the first Yamani answered.

"I saw her," he said solemnly. "And her hair was fire. Yours is just dying embers." There was general mirth among the tribesmen as he spoke, and then among the others as Ilana translated his words.

"Max, they want an answer." Iliana reminded him as the laughter dwindled. She, and everybody else around the fire, looked at him expectantly. Slowly Max stood, and as he did, he prayed for wisdom like he had never prayed before.

"Friends," he began. "You asked us to forgive you, but you have no need of our forgiveness. Your attack on us six months ago was provoked by others, and fueled by ignorance." He watched their expressions closely in the flickering firelight as Ilana translated. Some of the warriors remained stoic, while others seemed visibly relieved. "Rather, all mankind, white or brown, is in need of the forgiveness of that Great Spirit who plucked us from your midst."

Plucked us from your midst? Max thought. *Where did that come from? Shakespeare?*

"All of us have offended Him, and all of us deserve His righteous wrath. And yet, in His infinite mercy, He offered His Son as a sacrifice, pouring His wrath out on Him instead." Again, there were mixed reactions from the group.

Better get to the matter at hand.

"You have come to us for help, and as those who have been forgiven by the Great Spirit, we must help our fellow man. Let us confer among ourselves, and we will tell you our plan."

And he truly hoped that by the next day there would be a plan to tell them.

CHAPTER 4

THE BEST LAID PLANS

Five of the six Yamani warriors disappeared into the night. One stayed behind in order to get information to the tribe, should that be necessary. He sat in a corner and went to sleep while Max, Ilana, and Ray put their heads together to figure out what to do.

"Clearly we're going to have to go the Emerald Island," Max began. "We have to figure out where this attack came from and why, and that is where the answer will most likely be found. The question is, how do we get there?"

"I could fly you there, but I doubt the Shadow People have built a landing strip," Ray quipped.

"That means we will have to go the same way they did–by boat."

"Right," agreed Ilana. "Now, the question is, who should go?"

"Well, you and I are a given." said Max. "However long the Shadow People have been separated from their kin, their language is still bound to be basically the same. Whoever we find there, I'll need you to translate for me."

"Count me in!" exclaimed Ray.

"I don't know," Max said, thoughtfully.

"What, just because I'm the old guy I don't get to have any fun?"

"Trust me, Ray, there's nobody I'd rather have by my side in this situation. But, I think we may need somebody here who can bring in the cavalry if things get dicey."

"You mean swoop in with my plane again?"

"I was thinking more of some of the soldiers in my martial arts classes. And that brings up another question that's nagging at the back of my mind."

"What's that?"

"The Shadow People have lived peacefully separated from the other tribes for years."

"For centuries," Ilana corrected.

"Right. And they left because they couldn't stand all the fighting. Why, all of a sudden, do they decide to attack, unprovoked, the very people they left because they wanted peace?"

"What are you getting at?" asked Ray.

"I'm just saying, they may have been provoked by something–or someone."

"Not by the Yamani!" Ilana exclaimed. "You heard them, they had nothing to do with it.

"And I believe them. But that just makes the mystery even greater.

"Owanalehe." Ilana almost whispered the name. "He disappeared a while ago, and now this."

"Right," said Max. "And remember, when he tried to do us in back there in the jungle. He wasn't acting alone; he was put up to it by our friend Diego, who was working for Santana at the time–and for all we know he still is."

"Diego's grandmother was Yamani, from the Rock People," added Ilana

"So he is familiar with Yamani ways," Max mused. "And, if I remember correctly, Emídio Santana himself has more than a passing knowledge of the Yamani."

"That's right," agreed Ilana. "The Santana family has always been very involved in Yamani affairs...for all the wrong reasons."

There was a pause as everybody put the pieces together in their minds. Finally Max spoke. "It's just a hunch, but I do know this... we haven't heard anything from our friend Emídio Santana, or his lackey Diego, ever since my mother gave him a tongue-lashing in front of the whole army."

Ray grinned at the memory.

"I don't believe for a minute that they have repented of their evil ways and gone into basket weaving or some other benign profession."

Ilana snorted.

"So," continued Max, "my point is, our friend Santana is still out there, and up to no good, and there's more than a slight chance that he is somehow involved in all this. And if we go off in search of Icxi Xahn, someone needs stay back and keep an eye on Santana and Diego. Ray, that's where you come in."

Ray agreed, albeit reluctantly. "I guess I can talk to Cascavel, and put out some feelers to see if there is anything going on there. But at the very least we should stay in touch. We can use a two-way radio I fixed up a few years ago."

"Ray, you never cease to amaze me," said Max, shaking his head. He wondered how many other gadgets his friend had found and repaired since his arrival on Cabrito. "So it's settled," he continued. "Ray will stay here, and Ilana and I will go to the island. We'll send word to the Yamani to provide us with canoes and a few warriors to accompany us, and leave first thing in the morning."

Ilana stood to wake the warrior who had remained behind and give him the message, when another voice piped up.

"I'm going too." All heads turned to where Mary Sue had been sitting by herself in a corner, twirling her hair. So intent had the three been on their plans that they had completely forgotten their American guest.

"You can't be serious!" exclaimed Max. "Do you know what's out there? There's thick jungle, savage In..." Ilana cleared her throat. "Er...hostile indigenous people, snakes, wild animals..."

"I don't care," said Mary Sue, firmly. "I am not letting you go out there by yourself."

You can't handle staying in a house on Santo Expedito. What makes you think you can deal with the jungle? That's what Max wanted to say. But, seeing from the determined expression on her face that it would make no difference, he kept silent.

CHAPTER 5

OF MAX AND FRIENDS

Fog shrouded the beach as the small band set out for Emerald Island early Monday morning. Besides Max, Ilana, and Mary Sue, there were three young Yamani warriors–one representative from each sept of the tribe. They travelled in two long dug-out canoes, Ilana, Mary Sue, and one of the warriors in one, and Max and the remaining two warriors in the other.

Mary Sue was not especially pleased with this arrangement, nor was she happy with much else that had happened that morning. In the pre-dawn darkness Ray had taken her back to Bernadinho's house to change. Meanwhile, Max raided Ray's military surplus stash. When Mary Sue returned, Max was dressed in camouflage fatigues, his face covered with black and green paint. A machete in a leather case was strapped to his back, and a canvass knap-sack–containing radio equipment and other miscellaneous sup-plies–was slung over his shoulder.

Mary Sue, on the other hand, was wearing a crisp blue blouse and navy culottes. White tennis shoes completed the ensemble.

"Really?" Max asked. "You're planning on traipsing through the jungle in that?"

"Well, Maxwell Sherman," she said in her lecture voice, "what did you expect me to wear..."

Her voice trailed off as she saw Ilana standing behind him. The native girl sported the same dress she had been wearing as she and Max had scrambled pel-mel through the jungle just ahead of a howling horde of Yamanis. It was made from the skin of a jungle cat called an *onça pintada,* although the spots caused many to confuse it with a leopard. Her face, arms, and legs were painted in the camouflage of the tribal hunters. It was different in form from the Green Beret-style camouflage paint Max wore, but the purpose and net result were the same.

"I... I do not approve of this!" Mary Sue huffed. "What she is wearing is totally inappropriate!"

"For where we are going, what she is wearing is much more appropriate than your–whatever that is."

"Why, Max..."

Max was not about to endure another lesson. Not now. "Listen, Mary Sue–after fifteen minutes in the jungle, you're going to wish you were wearing something less...balloon-like. Now, you have a choice. You can accept the reality of what we are doing, or you can stay here and wait for us to come back. Your pick."

Max was secretly hoping she would choose the latter option, but instead she plopped herself back into seat of the VW and sat there in pouty silence until they arrived at the beach.

Now, as the sleek dugout canoes knifed through the choppy waves, Max glanced over at his girlfriend. Her long blonde hair was soaking wet and matted to her head. Her clothes were drenched. She huddled in the middle of the canoe, obviously miserable, and yet her jaw was set and her brow was furrowed–she was stubbornly determined to follow through with her decision. Despite the headache it was causing him, Max couldn't help but admire her for that.

At the bow of the same canoe sat Ilana, her arms glistening as she helped to row. Beneath the black war paint her eyes shone with a sense of adventure. She leaned forward, eagerly peering into the fog. To Max, the contrast between the two women could not have been greater, and the one he called his girlfriend came up seriously lacking.

The two way radio in Max's canvas backpack crackled to life, interrupting his thoughts. *"Nursing Home, Maxie Pie. Nursing Home, Maxie Pie. Do you read me? Over."* They had let Ray pick the call signs, which had been a mistake.

"Talk to me, Ray. Over"

"Everything OK out there, Maxie Pie? Over."

"So far so good." Max replied, ignoring the dig. "I think we are about half way. Ocean's a little rough, but nothing these Yamani guys can't handle. Over."

"Good. What about 'Jungle Princess'? Over."

"Ilana is fine. Over."

"And 'Blond Battle Axe'? Over."

Max cast a furtive glance at Mary Sue. Thankfully, she didn't seem to have heard over the sound of the waves. He held the radio up to his mouth and hissed, "She's miserable, and this is the *last* time I let you pick out the call signs. Over and out." He placed the radio back into the knapsack. Looking up, he found he could just make out the cliffs of Emerald Island. He wondered what they would find there. What kind of reception would they get from the Shadow People? What remained of Icxi Xahn? What had provoked this sudden attack on the Yamani people?

These questions and more swirled in his head as they drew inexorably closer to the forbidding cliffs.

A man clad head-to-toe in black stood at the edge of a cliff on Esmeralda, looking over the ocean in the direction of Cabrito.

With steady hands he held a pair of high-powered binoculars to his eyes and watched as the two canoes approached the island. On his shoulder, a patch depicted a lightning bolt in a clenched fist.

After a few minutes he put down the binoculars and turned to another, identically-dressed man a short distance behind him.

"Sergeant, get *señor* Santana on the radio. Tell him we have company, and that we await his instructions."

CHAPTER 6

OFTEN GO AWRY

James M. Rockwell sat at his desk in the office of the Cabrito installation of the Sherman Pharmaceutical Group, Incorporated. In front of him were stacks of paperwork: inventory lists, local permits, employment records–all things that made his managerial heart sing. It was Monday morning, and it promised to be another very profitable week.

The word "profitable" could aptly describe these last six months on Cabrito–if one discounted the little hiccup involving his CEO's wayward son, Max. Since then, things had been going swimmingly. And, truth be told, even that event, though quite stressful at the time, had netted him the services of Ilana, who had proven to be quite an efficient administrative assistant. She had originally been hired to be the liaison between SPGI and the native peoples, but after the events of six months earlier, the Yamani had proven illusive at best. There was also the added concern of Ilana's father Ray for his daughter's physical safety. But the vivacious young woman–raised in the jungle and educated in America–had proven to be such an asset that he had expanded her duties to include labor relations. Her winning personality and powers of persuasion had contributed to a very smooth launch of SPGI's Cabrito operations.

James was a little mystified as to the reasons for her sudden request for time off, but saw no reason not to agree. He suspected it had something to do with Max, and smiled as he pictured the two of them relaxing on one of Cabrito's beautiful beaches.

As he absentmindedly smoothed down an imaginary wisp of hair over his shiny head and prepared to make a serious dent in his in-box, there was a knock on the door. Without waiting for an answer, the door swung open and three soldiers walked in. James could tell by their uniforms that the one in the middle was in charge, and his two companions were the "muscle". All three of them were heavily armed. They stomped stiffly to the middle of the office and stood facing him.

"Please, come in," offered James, letting just a hint of sarcasm tinge his voice. Though taken by surprise, he had no intention of being intimidated by his new guests.

"*Senhor* James Rockwell, we are here, by order of the *presidente*, to escort you from the premises of the *Companhia Farmaceutica do Povo*."

"The People's Pharmaceutical Company? I'm sorry, I think you must have the wrong address. This is Sherman Pharmaceutical Group, Incorporated." He indicated the company logo on the wall.

"Was," replied the soldier curtly. "As of today, it is being repossessed by the people of Cabrito." He pulled a piece of paper from his breast pocket, unfolded it, and began to read:

Whereas SPGI has been guilty of gross exploitation of the Cabritan people...(James reflected on how the salary he paid was half-again as much as the national average)...*and whereas SPGI has hired people known to be enemies of the people...*(that could only mean Ilana, James realized)...*it has been decreed that the assets of SPGI on the island of Cabrito be returned to the people from whom they were taken, and that all foreign SPGI personnel* (which, James knew, consisted of exactly one person–himself) *remove themselves from Cabritan territory at the earliest opportunity. Signed, the hon-*

orable Osvaldo Ferraz, president of Cabrito, protector of the sur-rounding islands, etc. etc. etc.

Though boiling inside, James put on his broadest smile. He leaned back in his chair and spread his arms expansively. "*Meus caros amigos,* this is all some big misunderstanding. I'll call the *casa branca* right now and clear this all up." He reached for the phone, but before he could pick up one of the soldiers swept it from the desk. It clattered to the floor and broke open. James looked down at the phone, then up at the three soldiers.

"Well…" he said slowly, "It would appear you just broke the people's phone."

There was not even the hint of a smile from the soldiers. The leader spoke.

"*Senhor* Rockwell, we are not here to argue with you. You will leave the premises of your own volition, or we were remove you by force. Also, we have a warrant for the arrest of one Ilana Sand."

"Oh what bad luck!" exclaimed James with all the feigned sincerity he could muster. "She took a personal day today. If I hear from her, I'll tell her you stopped by."

Again, no reaction. James realized that there would be no talking these men out of their mission.

"And so, gentlemen, I bid you good day," he said finally, standing up and grabbing his briefcase. He was not about to let it or its contents be commandeered by "the people". With nothing else to do, he bowed slightly to the soldiers and left the office, whistling as he went.

Outside the building, workers were busy putting up a huge banner which read "Cabritan businesses, owned by the Cabritan people!" There were reporters on hand, but thankfully they were too busy taking pictures of the sign to pay attention to him. Several soldiers were stationed nearby, and there was a podium being set up.

So old Ferraz is going to hold a press conference about how he expelled the evil gringo. Too bad I didn't tape the speech he gave at our welcoming banquet. Then, as an afterthought… *I wonder what his cut of this whole operation is.*

Shaking his head, James got into his car and drove quietly away. When he found a secluded spot near a public park he pulled over, opened his briefcase, and reached for his satellite-phone. This problem would be resolved simply. He would talk to Regina, Regina would talk to George Santana, and everything would be back to normal–probably by tomorrow.

James dialed the number, waited for the secretary in New York to pick up, then identified himself and asked for the CEO. The ensuing conversation lasted less than five minutes, and when James Rockwell closed the phone his face was pale, his hands were shaking, and all semblance of nonchalance had disappeared.

It was around 9 am when the two canoes reached Emerald Island. The waves had been high, but nothing the skilled Yamani warriors couldn't handle. Finding a place to put to shore, however, proved to be a difficulty. The rock cliffs emerged abruptly from the ocean and continued straight up for several hundred feet. Max knew he would have no trouble scaling the walls, and he would most likely be joined by the three Yamani warriors and Ilana. He also knew that Mary Sue wouldn't make it more than three feet. Then there was the question of what to do with the canoes.

After a few minutes of searching they found a sandy alcove surrounded by high cliffs. Dragging the canoes onto the little beach, they took stock of the situation. Lighting a fire was out of the question as there was no dry wood to be found anywhere. Their position was secure at that point–it was already high tide, so there was no danger of their little refuge disappearing beneath the waves– but there was still no way for them to get up to the jungle.

Max, Ilana and the warriors held a short conference and it was decided that Max would take one of the canoes and explore the coast, looking for a way up the rocks. The others would wait for his return. Max was reluctant to leave, but, under the circumstances, he saw no other option. Convincing himself that the three warriors would be able to provide sufficient protection for the two women, he set out.

Predictably, Mary Sue was not happy with the arrangement, but by this time Max was immune to her protests.

As he pushed the canoe out into the waves once more, the drizzle stopped and the sun peeked out from behind the clouds. Max paddled along the cliffs for some time. After about an hour of searching he had found a few other alcoves like the ones where his companions were docked, but nothing more interesting than that.

Somewhat discouraged, Max considered turning back. His arms were tired from paddling, and as he came upon another alcove he decided to stop and rest. Pulling the canoe up to the shore, he got out and stretched out on the sand, eyes closed, letting the sun warm him through.

A few minutes later he opened his eyes, and then sat up in astonishment at what he saw. The alcove was not much different from the one where his companions were waiting–high rock cliffs surrounding a sandy beachhead–but Max now saw something that set this particular alcove apart: someone a long time ago had carved a stairway into the face of the cliff. It began at the sand to Max's right, and curved up over his head, winding back and forth, following the contours of the rock. Max squinted his eyes to see where it ended.

Is that what I think it is?

He stood up and walked over where the staircase met the sand. After examining it for safety, he began to climb, moving gingerly from step to slippery step. It had obviously been carved into the granite wall decades, maybe centuries ago, and there were places where it was quite worn away. Was this a Yamani construction? Part of some long-forgotten European settlement? A pirate cave?

Max continued to climb. At one point his foot slipped on the slick stone and for a moment he thought he would plummet to the sand below. Regaining his balance, he continued on.

Max estimated that he was roughly three hundred feet above the ground when he reached the end of the staircase. And just as he had suspected, he found himself at the entrance to a cave.

Producing a flashlight from the knapsack, Max clicked it on and stepped into the dark entrance. His eyes were met by a scene of decades-old chaos. Max counted six skeletons stretched out on the ground, still covered by tattered grey rags–clearly the remains of military uniforms. Multiple arrows protruded from now-vacant chest cavities. To his right, another skeleton slumped over a wooden table. It's bony right hand still gripped a rusted 9mm Lugar. Besides the arrows protruding from its empty shirt, there was an ugly dent in its skull.

It wasn't hard for Max to figure out what had happened here. The soldiers had taken refuge in the cave, and felt themselves secure from attack from the outside. Judging from the position of the bodies and accompanying arrows, however, it was clear that the attack had come from the dark recesses of the cave behind them.

Poor guys probably never knew what hit them, Max mused. He turned his attention to the remains slumped over the table. Because of his position, this one had probably seen what was happening, and had time to get out his weapon. Perhaps he had gotten off a shot or two, and maybe even scored a hit. That would explain why, after filling him with arrows, the attackers had thought it necessary to bash his head in.

Max shined his light once again over the bodies. On the right sleeve of each one was a band containing the unmistakable broken cross of the Third Reich.

"Nazis? What were you doing here?"

Turning his attention from the skeletal remains, he began to examine the other contents of the cave. A few empty crates were strewed about, obviously broken into and emptied by the attackers. Inching farther back into the darkness, he almost tripped over a very large, oblong box made of wood. Letting his light shine over its contours, Max found it to be similar in shape to a coffin. But if it were indeed a coffin, it had been made to carry an enormous cadaver–roughly half-again the size of any normal man, Max surmised. The wooden cover was leaning to one side of the box, and whatever had once occupied the space occupied it no longer.

Max's mind was filled with questions about the odd container, and what it had once held. However, there was work to be done, so he pushed them out of his head and returned to the opening of the cave.

The SPGI building in New York was one of those beautiful old skyscrapers, built back when architects envisioned such buildings as works of art and not the random collection of geometric shapes that characterizes modern high-rises. Of course it had not always been called the SPGI building, but for the past twenty years it had served as the center of operations for the Sherman family's ever-expanding enterprises.

From the outside, the top floor of the building actually resembled a cathedral, with high, pointed windows through which sunlight streamed in to the center. Inside, the entire floor served as an enormous conference room. A gigantic, oblong mahogany table sat in the middle. It was here that Regina Sherman, under normal circumstances, held court for the board of SPGI.

These were not normal circumstances.

While on this particular Monday the SPGI board was gathered together as always, and while Regina Sherman occupied her usual place at the head of the table, she was not hearing reports of the expansion of SPGI interests around the globe. Instead, she was watching her life's work–and that of her late husband–crumble around her.

At the midway point of the vast conference table sat a wizened old man. His pockmarked face framed a cruel mouth which seemed to be turned up in a perpetual sneer. His eyes were black, bottomless pits.

Indeed, if eyes reflect the soul, looking into George Santana's eyes would give the impression that, in his case, there was no soul to be reflected.

Regina Sherman had just returned to the room after her phone conversation with James Rockwell, and now she glared at the old man. Her stare was as icy as ever, but the disturbing talk she had just had with James had left her reeling inside.

"So you see, Ms. Sherman," Santana continued with a voice that sounded like a weed-whacker in a gravel pit, "Santana Holdings, Ltd has been in quiet negotiations with SPGI stockholders and board members for quite some time."

Regina's stare turned to the other men and women around the table–many of whom had been personally groomed and prepared for their positions by her and her husband. One by one they looked away as her gaze bore down on them.

Traitors! She wondered just how much of his personal fortune Santana had spent to buy off each one.

"While we are grateful for your years of dedication to the company, a change is leadership is now in its best interests." The grating voice with its slight Portuguese accent came to a stop. There was a deathly pause that grew exponentially more uncomfortable as it continued.

"Out!" Regina's voice echoed throughout the hall, and everybody jumped. Even the gloating George Santana flinched. "All of you, out!" And despite the fact that she had just been effectively fired, everyone at the table scurried to vacate the conference room. Soon George Santana and Regina Sherman were alone.

Regina approached George, shaking with rage. "Perhaps you forget the little financial irregularities my husband discovered in his dealings with Santana Holdings. If you persist in this madness, I will go to the papers first thing tomorrow morning." The threat had worked before, but today it seemed empty, even as she made it.

George Santana's face took on an expression of something nearing pity. "I'm afraid it's too late for that, my dear. When you read the paper tomorrow the headline will be about dreadful abuses carried out by SPGI employees against the helpless natives of a tiny island called Cabrito. I'm sure you've heard of it. In fact, unless I miss my guess, the urgent phone call you took just now was from one Mr. Rockwell, informing you of the government takeover of your facilities there, in response to said abuses. Am I right?"

Regina's stony silence was all the answer he got–and it was all he needed.

"I've been working on this little project for some time now. That unfortunate incident between our respective offspring convinced me that the time had come to remove you–and whatever knowledge you may have of our financial dealing–from the picture. If you want my advice, find a nice little retirement community in Boca where you can enjoy your golden years, and pray that your stupid son lives long enough to give you grandchildren. Now..." he rose to his full height–which still put him a good foot and a half shorter than the woman in front of him, "...you have fifteen minutes to get out of my building before I call security and have you thrown out."

MISSIONARY MAX AND THE JUNGLE PRINCESS

44

CHAPTER 7

WHEN IN DOUBT, LISTEN TO THE GUYS WITH UZIS

Despite his irritation at not being allowed to go to Emerald Island with the others, Raymond Sand was taking his "home guard" assignment seriously. After dropping Max, Ilana, and Mary Sue off at the beach, his first stop had been the home of Cascavel–the street thug-turned-believer in Christ who had become a sort of right-hand man to Ray. Even if Ray did not share Cascavel's newfound faith, they both shared an intense loyalty to Missionary Max.

The older man had filled his wiry little friend in on the details of what was happening. Cascavel had been at the church service when the Yamani warriors showed up, so he was not too surprised. Like Ray, however, he was a little put-out that he had not been invited to go along. Ray managed to assuage his feelings by telling him that Missionary Max would greatly appreciate his work "behind the scenes."

Together, the two had decided that a wise course of action would be to call on their friend James Rockwell, manager of the Cabritan branch of the Sherman Pharmaceutical Group, Incorporated.

Because the CEO of SPGI was Max's mother, James was especially concerned with his well-being. In addition, he moved in high circles on Cabrito, and might have some sort of idea as to what was behind the recent unrest among the Yamani. At the very least he would be able to snoop around and get back to them.

As they pulled up to the SPGI building they noticed a large podium set up, and a crowd beginning to form. Soldiers were posted at either end of the platform. Then Ray saw the sign.

"This can't be good," he growled. He parked the Volkswagen and he and Cascavel casually walked toward the edge of the crowd.

Soon they saw President Ferraz approach the podium. Behind him Ray could see Emídio Santana sitting with a group of dignitaries. Ferraz began to read from a prepared speech.

"Fellow citizens of Cabrito. It is with great pride that I present to you the People's Pharmaceutical Company–owned and operated by the people of Cabrito!"

He paused, and after a moment's hesitation the crowd obliged with a smattering of applause.

"We were saddened to learn of the many abuses of SPGI–crimes against the citizens of this fair island. For this reason, we ordered our brave army to invade these premises–which they did, at great risk to themselves."

"Yeah, I bet that little bald guy in the office put up a big fight," Ray muttered.

"And now this factory, with all its installations, belongs to the people of Cabrito. I would like to personally thank our very own Emídio Santana, who has generously, and at his own expense, made it possible for operations to continue as usual."

More less-than-spontaneous applause, and Santana stood to acknowledge the crowd. President Ferraz stepped to one side, and Santana approached the podium.

There was a tugging at Ray's sleeve. It was Cascavel. "*Senhor* Raimundo, I think maybe we should leave before we get seen by somebody who recognizes us, no?" He jerked his head to where Emídio Santana was beginning his remarks.

Ray agreed, and they made their way to the parked taxi and headed back towards Ray's place.

As Ray drove, he tried to piece together what was happening. Why this sudden hostile takeover of SPGI? How did they expect to get away with it without incurring the wrath of the formidable Regina Sherman? Ray's one encounter with Max's mother on the runway had left him with the distinct impression that she was no woman to be trifled with.

Even more importantly, did this have anything to do with the recent happenings on Emerald Island? The events were too close together to be dismissed out of hand as mere coincidence.

They would still need to talk to James, Ray decided, but for now the thing to do was to radio Max and fill him in on these surprising developments. Perhaps Ilana would have some idea as to what was going on–although Ray was sure that if his daughter knew anything about it, she would have told him long ago.

Ray rounded the bend in the dirt road that led to his farm, and put on the brakes so hard Cascavel found himself scrunched up against the windshield. Grumbling something about crazy American drivers he regained his seat, and then looked over at Ray.

"Cascavel," Ray said quietly. "Don't make any sudden moves."

Cascavel followed the older man's gaze and froze. There, standing in the road in front of them, were two very large men. There was no way to continue without going over or through them–and the Uzi's they were both carrying made that an unattractive option.

"Raimundo, I…"

"Shut up!" Ray hissed.

"But Raimundo, you don't…"

Ray turned quickly to Cascavel. "If you don't shut your can I will kill you before those two get the chance," he hissed.

Cascavel shut his can.

The two men approached the little Volkswagen. "Can I help you gentlemen?" Ray asked, rolling down his window as they approached and trying to sound casual. The two men said nothing. Instead they went to opposite sides of the car and opened the back doors.

"Well," said Ray affably. "This is technically a taxi, but I'm afraid my meter isn't running right now…" He glanced in the rear-view mirror and saw the Uzis rested casually on the two men's laps. They were standard edition, and Ray knew that the magazines would be loaded with 9mm cartridges. "Then again, we can always make a special run. Where to, gentlemen?"

"Drive east," was the reply.

"Right, east," echoed the other.

"Listen to me Raimundo!" Cascavel pleaded in a low whisper. "I know these guys. They threatened to kill me once."

"What? When?"

"On the day I was waiting outside your house to...er...kill you."

"So...if they were threatening you back when you were a bad guy, that must mean..."

"It means we're the good guys," completed one of the large men in the back.

"Right, the good guys." came the ubiquitous echo.

Ray was having a hard time placing the accent. It wasn't Cabritan–but it also wasn't straight European Portuguese either. Cape Verde and the Azores were also out, so that left...

"Now drive." It was the first one again, interrupting Ray's process of elimination. "Someone has some very important things to tell you."

"Right, very important things." repeated his partner.

Ray drove. As they bounced over dirt roads away from Santo Expedito and up the ridge that hemmed in Cabrito's capital city, his mind worked overtime to get ahead of the situation.

Then it dawned on him. He had heard the same speech mannerisms in a thousand televised soccer games, novellas, and just about every popular song that invaded the airwaves. *Now...where would two Brazilian toughs with Uzis be taking us?*

His examination of the cave had revealed to Max that it continued a long way into the darkness. A light breeze coming from its dark recesses lead him to believe that there was some kind of opening at the other end, although he could discern no light in that direction.

The swastika-adorned, arrow-ridden skeletons interested him, and the giant coffin–if indeed that was what it was–had his curiosity up. If there had been more time he would have loved to explore further. For now, however, he needed to get back to the group. He had toyed briefly with the idea of bringing them back to the cave. At the very least it would provide them with shelter and a base of operations. Yet the gruesome fate of the German troops made him abandon that idea altogether. They would use the stairs to get to the top of the cliff, then scramble up the few remaining feet and strike off through the jungle. He knew he would feel more comfortable under the canopy of green than under who-knew-how-many feet of rock, and he was pretty sure Ilana and the Yamani warriors would feel the same way.

What will Mary Sue think of the plan? Max wondered as he carefully descended the stone steps to his canoe. And as he pushed off and began rowing with strong, even strokes, headed for the small alcove where he had left his friends, he came to the conclusion that it didn't really matter.

After about an hour of steady rowing, he pulled his canoe up to the tiny beach where he had left his friends.

It was empty.

Max jumped out of the canoe and sprinted ashore. Arriving at where they had originally come aground, he stopped short and gasped in horror. The bodies of the three Yamani who had accompanied them were sprawled on the sand. The waves lapped around their legs, tugging gently but insistently at their feathered anklets. All three of them had been shot. Blood soaked into the beach, and small wisps of red snaked into the water.

The sight of the lifeless forms brought waves of unwelcome memories crashing down over Max. Ever since his father had died back when he was a teenager he had felt like death was stalking him. This had only increased during his Green Beret days, where too many if his buddies–better men than he–had met untimely ends in Iraq, Afghanistan, and other, less publicized places. In those dark days he had often wished that death would stop it's incessant teasing and find him as well.

Thankfully, Jesus found him first. And yet, although Christianity allowed Max to put death into perspective, it didn't make it any more pleasant.

With great effort Max turned away from the bodies of his Yamani companions and began looking around for clues. Getting desperate here would not help anybody. Looking at the tracks in the sand, he could easily identify Mary Sue's tennis shoes, and the bare feet of Ilana. Intermingled with them were the prints of several boots–about eight pair, Max calculated. Something shiny caught his eye, and he bent down to pick up a spent shell casing. Max identified it as 7.62x51mm ammo, which meant that whoever these guys were, they were most likely carrying HK G36 assault rifles. Max had cross-trained with these particular weapons while on a mission in Serbia and knew power they packed.

Pocketing the shell casing, he examined the remaining tracks. He could see where the eight booted men had descended from the above, rapidly rappelling down the cliffs, taking the small party unawares. After eliminating the Yamani warriors, they had returned up the cliff, this time with the Ilana and Mary Sue. With great relief he found no evidence that either of the young women had shared the warriors' fate.

Scanning the rock wall, Max saw something flicking in the wind about ten feet above him. He jumped up and grabbed onto a small crack in the face of the rock, pulling himself up by his hands and arms. Once he found a small toehold, he reached up with his free hand and plucked the tiny object from the rock. Max smiled grimly. It was a small shard of *onça* skin, and it had to have been left there on purpose.

Leave it to Ilana to keep her head in this situation.

Without a second's hesitation Max began to climb, hand over hand, up the face of the cliff.

CHAPTER 8

UNEMPLOYMENT BENEFITS

Regina Sherman was without a job, but she was by no means destitute. Besides her regular bank accounts and her many properties and investments, she had money squirreled away in places George Santana wouldn't dream of looking. She and her late husband hadn't built SPGI into a multinational pharmaceutical powerhouse by being stupid or naïve.

Nor had they built it by taking defeat easily. Pulling her fur coat close to her in the December cold, she walked swiftly to the parking garage with the box of personal effects she had managed to salvage from her office. Her mind raced through possible next steps. All her employees were now her *former* employees. None of them would be under any obligation to do her any favors.

The one employee who she trusted absolutely was stranded, incommunicado, on the island of Cabrito, as was her only close family member.

Regina ran through all her US associates one by one, discarding each as potentially compromised by George Santana; she was beginning to grasp at straws. She opened the door of her Bentley Continental GT, sat down, and gripped the wheel.

Get a hold of yourself, Regina! she ordered, with the same finality with which she would order her subordinates. *You just need to think.*

And think she did. Analytically, calmly, she went over all the details, discarding options as they came to her. Finally, she arrived at one conclusion. She had to get in touch with Max. He was probably traipsing around the jungle with his native girlfriend. She had never believed for a moment that there was nothing between them; even though she was a high-powered executive she was still a woman, and she could tell when there was an emotional connection between two people. Somehow she needed to get him connected to James, and together the three of them could get to the bottom of this and expose George Santana for the fraud that he was. How, she had not the slightest idea. What was important now was consolidating her base. Every ally would be important.

Back when Max had first talked about going into the Army, Regina Sherman had opposed the idea with every fiber in her body. Yet, she had a mind any military strategist would envy. Max may have inherited the name and bull-headed stubbornness of his infamous Civil War relative, but even Regina's late husband had concurred that his gift for analytical thinking had come from his mother's side of the family. And though mutual stubbornness had driven mother and son apart over the years, she was confident that if they got their heads together, they could put a stop to this nonsense.

But how to contact him? In their brief conversation James had said that he was unaware of Max's whereabouts. And now even James was not an option. Regina thought back to when Max had left the Army and moved to Greensborough, New York, to work for a construction company. She had virtually disowned her only son by that time, and had never visited him there. Still, she was not unfamiliar with that part of the country–she and her husband had been regulars at the Saratoga races and had a little vacation cabin not far from there. Greensborough would be a good place to start. She would check first with the construction company where Max had worked. She found the name and address on her smartphone, then keyed the coordinates into her GPS.

Tires squealed on the pavement and the Bentley roared out of the parking garage. Christmas shoppers at Harold Square gawked as the she blew past them. Taking corners as if they were gentle curves, Regina sped through the streets of Manhattan, weaving in and out of traffic until finally finding her way to the George Washington bridge. She crossed the bridge to the Turnpike, where she finally gave the powerful vehicle permission to fulfill the purpose for which it had been designed. The pistons whirred, the engine sang, the wheels whined on the pavement, and Regina Sherman sped like an arrow through the foothills of the Adirondack mountains towards Greensborough.

Pistons coughing, engine groaning, and wheels sinking into mud, the yellow "*Transporte Raimundo*" Volkswagen climbed laboriously up the steep ridge to the east of Santo Expedito. The engine ran hot, and the wheels bumped in and out of the large ruts formed years earlier by heavy trucks–part of a failed logging venture. As if to mock the very idea of deforestation, the jungle grew tall and thick on either side of the road. Ray carefully steered the little Volkswagen around huge pot-holes, at times having to forge side trails in the jungle underbrush.

Inside the vehicle silence reigned. Ray concentrated on his driving, and Cascavel concentrated on trying to concentrate on Ray's driving, and not on the two heavily-armed men in the back seat. These, for their part, remained perfectly still, seemingly unperturbed by the jarring bumps and unpredictable starts and stops.

How bad must roads be in Brazil if this doesn't faze them? Ray wondered as he ground the transmission down to first gear in order to pass over a particularly large bump.

After what seemed like forever the car crested the ridge and began its descent down the other side. The descent was only slightly more bearable now that gravity was working with instead of against them.

Ray was beginning to think they were going to follow the trail all the way up to the little fishing communities on the north side of the island, when without warning one of the men in the back ordered "Stop!"

"Right, stop," echoed his partner.

Ray pulled the VW over to the side of the trail, and at the indication of his two passengers, got out. Cascavel was right behind him.

"Now you follow me." Again the order from the man with the Uzi.

"Right, follow him." Again the repetition from his identically armed colleague.

Without pausing to make sure his order was being carried out, the first man plunged into the jungle. Ray followed, and saw that they were on a trail of sorts. They wound their way, single-file, deeper and deeper into the jungle. Ray had taken to thinking of his two "passengers" as "Brazilian Number One" and "Brazilian Number Two." As they pushed deeper and deeper into the jungle, Brazilian Number One was in front, then Ray, then Cascavel, then Brazilian Number Two. Ray was packing his .45, as was his habit, and the two men had made no attempt to search him. Still, he knew there would be little sense in trying to use it. He might get one of them, but not both.

Besides, Ray had a feeling that, wherever they were going, they were about to get some answers to questions that had been nagging them since Sunday, and he didn't want to miss that opportunity. Going out in a blaze of glory would have to wait.

The green canopy blocked out the sun, so that Ray–who normally had a keen sense of direction–soon lost all notion of where they were. All he knew was that they continued to descend. It all began to remind him of Vietnam, and *that* was something he would have preferred not to remember. He tried some small talk.

"Great weather for a stroll." Nothing.

They continued on in silence punctuated by the calls of exotic birds and the crunching of leaves under their feet for about an hour. Then, just as he was beginning to despair of ever leaving this green oblivion, Ray noticed that the air was becoming a little cooler. A small breeze was penetrating the trees, which, for their part, were beginning to thin out, ever so slightly.

Behind him, Cascavel sniffed. *"O mar!"* he whispered. "The sea!"

At that instant they broke out of the jungle. Ray shielded his eyes from the sudden onslaught of sunlight. Squinting, he looked around him. They were on the edge of a beautiful lagoon. A beach of pure white sand separated the crystal-blue water from the dark green of the forest. On the other side of the lagoon a small, tree-lined channel led out to the ocean.

The water looked so cool and inviting after their long trek that Ray had an urge to run and dive in. Only the presence of their heavily-armed companions checked his desire. Despite Cascavel's claim that they were "the good guys," Ray continued to be wary of them.

To their right was a quaint little cabana. Its walls were made of rough-hewn logs, and it was topped with a roof of palm leaves. It was set up on stilts and extended out over the water. A veranda faced the channel that led to the ocean. A wooden ramp let from the beach to the door on the end closest to them.

The two armed men–who looked remarkably out of place in such a picturesque setting–motioned Ray and Cascavel towards the house. Before they reached the door they heard a female voice from inside.

"Please come in."

Opening the door and stepping inside, Ray and Cascavel found themselves in a simple yet elegantly furnished living room. Wicker furniture surrounded a large, circular carpet. To their right a portion of the room was used as a kitchen, separated by a little bar, complete with three bamboo stools. A couple old photos graced the wall. In the corner was an old TV with rabbit-ear antennae.

At the far end of the room, opposite where Ray and Cascavel stood, was an open door where a tall woman with golden blond hair falling down in waves to her shoulders was standing. She was the picture of statuesque poise.

"Welcome, Raimundo. It is a pleasure to finally meet you." She spoke in the same lyrical Brazilian dialect of the Portuguese language–refined over the centuries from its harsh Eurpoean origins by the gentle sculpting of the indigenous and African tongues.

Ray had never met the woman before him but there wasn't a man in all of Cabrito who didn't know who she was.

"Dona Francesca," he said, with as much aplomb as he could manage on such short notice. "To what do we owe the pleasure of your...ah...unorthodox invitation?"

The woman gave a slight, almost girlish giggle at the crusty American's attempt at formality. Then she was serious again. "Come in," she said. "We have much to talk about."

Max and Cascavel stepped into the room. Behind them the two suits took their places, one on either side of the door. Seeing them made Ray stop.

"Now hold on," he said. Francesca turned to look at him. "Before we go any farther, I want some explanation." Ray's civilized veneer proved to be very short-lived indeed. "Why in the blazes was it necessary for these to thugs to carjack us and bring us all the way out here?"

"Right. All the way out here," echoed Cascavel. Ray shot him a dirty look.

Francesca gave them both a thin smile. "There will be time for detailed explanations later," she said. "For now you might want to thank my loyal bodyguards Itamar and Inácio. In all probability, they just saved your lives."

CHAPTER 9

REDECORATING

The ancient Portuguese estate–or *casarão*–that Ray and Ilana called home had clearly seen better days. Added to the natural course of decay was the fact that Ray had lived there alone for several years, and this had accelerated rather than delayed the process of deterioration. Yet, in the short months that had passed since the arrival of Ilana, a subtle transformation could be detected. It started with a general cleaning. Decades-worth of dust was removed from floors, walls, and fixtures. Cupboards and furniture were repaired and organized. Dirty dishes were cleaned and stacked. Then amenities such as curtains and carpets began to appear. The smell of new paint could be detected. First it was the occasional touch-up, then entire rooms shed their drab coatings and put on cheery pastels.

Ray's first reaction to his daughter's civilizing touch was to grumble that his house was looking too "girly." On more than one occasion, however, when Max had come to visit he had found the old soldier involved in some remodeling project. One morning he even found him planting flowers in the front yard. That had been awkward for both of them, and they never mentioned it afterwards.

While there was still much to be done, Ilana was happy with the changes she had been able to make so far.

And she would have been horrified to see what happened when the Lightning Force came.

Dressed head-to-toe in black–each one sporting the lightning-fist insignia–twenty men burst through the windows and doors, assault rifles at the ready, sending shards of glass and wood flying in every direction. Like dark shadows they raced from room to room, overturning furniture, breaking fixtures, and generally creating chaos. Finally it became evident that nobody was home. While one of the troops radioed this information, the commander removed his hood. He was a big man with a wide face and small, cruel eyes that darted back and forth, missing no details.

One of the troopers ran up to him and saluted smartly. "Lieutenant Stromm, there is a barn out back, filled with old cars, and a biplane."

"Take a detail and slash the tires. All of them."

"Yes sir!" The soldier scrambled to carry out the order, and Stromm continued to analyze his surroundings. Eliminating the old man had been their main objective. Stromm was used to achieving his objectives, and since his target was not where he expected him to be, he needed to find where he was.

"Sir, you need to see this." It was the same trooper he had ordered to slash the tires. Stromm followed him through the back of the house and into the barn. Momentarily he marveled at the collection of antique cars. Then he turned his attention to his trooper, who was removing a tarp. Underneath was a radio set.

As Stromm bent down to examine it, a voice crackled over the speaker: "*Max to Nursing Home. Come in, Nursing Home.*"

There was a pause, and then again, more urgently:

"*Come in, Nursing Home. Ray, do you read me? Come in Ray!*"

Despite the crackling connection, the *ianqui* accent was unmistakable. This could only be the other American–the one another task force was supposed to be rounding up this morning. Stromm frowned. The voice on the other end sounded desperate, but the fact that there *was* a voice on the other end meant that somehow he had eluded capture and was still at large. Commander Stromm looked at the receiver thoughtfully. What was the name again? Max, that was it. He put the receiver to his mouth and clicked it on.

"Mister Max, I regret to inform zat your friend is no longer vis us. You also vil be found und dealt vith. It is only matter of time."

There was a pause at the other end, then a *click* and the line went dead. Stromm smiled. *Now he will panic.*

Max looked at his radio, stunned. What had happened to Ray? Who was that German voice on the other end? What did "no longer with us" mean? One thing he knew: calling in the cavalry had ceased to be an option.

Once again Max willed his nerves to calm down and forced himself to work through the situation rationally. Scaling the cliff had taken the remainder of the morning. Now he was standing on top. Behind him stretched the ocean. The main island of Cabrito was a dark bump on the horizon. In front of him: dense green jungle. And somewhere in that jungle was Ilana...

...and Mary Sue, he reminded himself.

One thing was clear: whatever was going on with Ray back on Cabrito, there was absolutely nothing Max could do about it. His best bet was to catch up with the party that had captured the girls and go from there. The place where they had entered the jungle was obvious. Whoever these men were, they either had no jungle skills or were unconcerned with concealing their tracks. He would have the advantage of speed, since there was one of him and, as best as he could calculate, about thirteen of them–two of whom were unwilling parties.

Max put the radio back into his knapsack. It was useless to him now, but who knew whether or not it might come in handy later. With jaw set in grim determination he fastened the knapsack, drew the machete from its leather case and plunged into the green undergrowth.

The luxury yacht *Lua Negra* was the pride of the Atlantic. Russian crime bosses and Silicon Valley executives all had their "bath toys," but their "power of acquisition" was minuscule compared to that of the Santana family. The floating palace boasted, among other amenities, two helipads, an Olympic sized pool, indoor soccer and basketball courts, and four observation decks.

Inside, the *Lua Negra* was the definition of opulence. It contained several luxury suites, each one more lavish than the last, culminating in the master-suite, which was a mini-palace in itself, featuring an enormous bed facing a cinema-sized movie screen. At the touch of a button the ceiling would open and allow the occupants of the room to contemplate the night sky.

Adjacent to the master-suite was an office that made the executive headquarters of the *Casa Branca* seem like a cubicle in comparison. Much of the front wall was occupied by a screen, only slightly smaller than the one in the bedroom. Bullet-proof windows formed a half-circle in the back of the spacious room, giving an unrestricted view of the ocean. Curtains could be drawn at the push of a button should the occupants of the office desire privacy.

In front of the windows sat an ostentatiously enormous mahogany desk. Giving the desk an even more imposing aspect was the fact that it was set up on a dais. On the floor in front of the dais were two chairs upholstered with leather. The position of the chairs relative to the desk was calculated to intimidate.

Presidente Ozvaldo Ferraz was duly intimidated. He had thought his duties for the day would end with the speech at the pharmaceutical plant that morning, but at the last minute Santana had "requested" his presence on the *Lua Negra*. Now he wished he were anywhere else.

He always hated trips to the *Lua Negra*, and this one was no exception. It always seemed to confirm his suspicion that his position as *presidente* was truly insignificant. Plus, this extravagant workspace always gave him a serious case of "office envy."

And now, adding insult to injury, he was forced to listen as Santana lectured him about the failure of his army regulars to arrest Ilana that morning.

Seated next to him, and equally uncomfortable, was General Manfred Krugel, commander of the Lightning Force. Krugel was not accustomed to reporting failure. His army–hand-picked from the best mercenaries money could buy and dedicated to the protection of Santana family interests around the globe–was very efficient at its job. Yet he too was being reamed out by Santana over their failure to eliminate Raymond Sand and Maxwell Sherman.

On the screen behind them flickered the images of two of the Lightning Force's division leaders: Stromm and LaRue.

"There was simply nobody home, sir." It was Lieutenant Stromm. "We did find a communication device, and intercepted a message from *Herr* Sherman to *Herr* Sand."

"We had ze same misfortune," echoed LaRue. "We ransacked ze apartment, but it was obvious that *monsieur* Max has–how do the English put it–flown ze poop."

"Krugel?" Santana looked at his commander inquiringly. "Do you have an explanation for this?"

Ferraz smiled inwardly. Next to these two idiots, his own performance that morning seemed stellar.

Krugel shifted uncomfortably in his chair. "Sir I..." suddenly he put his hand to his ear. "Hold on–I have an incoming from Lieutenant Sanchez on Esmeralda Island. Yes...go ahead lieutenant."

There was a long pause, then Krugel looked up and smiled. "Sir, I am happy to report the target called Ilana has been apprehended by Sanchez' unit on Esmeralda Island."

Santana looked pointedly at Ferraz: "Well, it seems that the Lightning Force has made up for the deficiencies of your regular army, wouldn't you say, Mr. President?"

A string of potent curses went through the *presidente's* head, but outwardly he looked at Krugel and smiled warmly. "Congratulations to your men on the capture of a girl," he said, his voice dripping sarcasm. He turned back to Santana. "It would appear, however, that the main targets, the ones called "Max" and "Ray," have escaped them."

"This is unfortunate," rejoined Krugel, "but according to Sanchez this Ilana arrived with a party in two boats, accompanied by three Yamani warriors, one white male in military-style fatigues and another young female. The Yamani warriors offered resistance and were liquidated At this moment the two women are in Sanchez' custody. The white male is unaccounted for, but presumably on Esmeralda Island. From the description, it is also safe to say that the unidentified male is this Maxwell Sherman."

"Ah, you see!" It was Pierre LaRue. "Certainly it is only a matter of time before zis 'Missionary Max' is captured. He is, as the English say, 'up ze creek wizout ze fiddle.'"

Once again Osvaldo Ferraz saw his chance. "Your elite squad has shot primitive natives with automatic weapons, apprehended two women, and all the while the most dangerous man continues to elude them. Bravo!" He stood up and clapped his hands slowly once, twice, three times.

Both Stromm and LaRue started to protest, but stopped short when Emídio brought his fist down on the desk with such force that everybody–even Conchita–jumped. Ferraz sat down quickly. "Maxwell Sherman cannot be underestimated!" he roared.

Right, reflected Ferraz. *He kicked your tail in front of five hundred Yamanis not too long ago.*

"Inform Lieutenant Sanchez that until further notice his primary mission is to find and neutralize Missionary Max," Santana continued.

"And the original mission?"

"Trust me, until you get rid of this Missionary Max, the original mission will always be in jeopardy. Have I made myself clear?"

"Perfectly!" exclaimed Krugel, rising to his feet.

Santana directed his attention to the screen. "As for you two, combine your units and look for Raymond Sand. Stromm, you mentioned a barn full of cars earlier...

"*Und* an airplane..." Stromm added helpfully. Emídio winced, as if from a painful memory. Then he stood and addressed his guests.

"Gentlemen, I cannot emphasize enough the importance of rounding up Mr. Sherman and Mr. Sand. The success of our plans will always be in question until these two dangerous elements have been eliminated. Now go."

Krugel stood and saluted smartly. "We will not fail you sir!" he said, and exited the room. The TV screen went blank and Santana busied himself with papers on his desk. He looked up to see Ferraz still sitting there in front of him.

"Why are you still here?"

"I thought..."

"You thought wrong. Get out."

Seething, Ferraz stood and left the room. He could feel Conchita's sneer following him out the door.

Back in the office, Santana sighed. "The next person I talk to better know where those troublemakers are," he muttered to nobody in particular.

Just then the phone rang, and Emídio picked up the receiver. "Hello Francesca. I can't talk right now." There was a pause. "No, I'm not planning on going to the house anytime soon. In fact, I will probably be on the boat all week long. Find something to do to keep yourself entertained, and please don't bother me. I'm *very* busy."

MISSIONARY MAX AND THE JUNGLE PRINCESS

CHAPTER 10

I'VE GOT YOUR NUMBER

Francesca placed her satellite phone on the table next to her and smiled triumphantly at Ray and Cascavel. "We aren't going to have to worry about Emídio being around for the next few days. We still need to be careful, but at least I won't have to make any appearances at public functions or at the mansion. Now, let's get back to comparing notes."

Ray and Cascavel were seated at the wooden bar separating the kitchen from the living area of the cabana, situated in the dream-like lagoon. Besides his obvious talents as a bodyguard, Inácio, it turned out, was no slouch as a chef. He made them a delicious lunch consisting of fish (Ray wasn't sure what kind, and was too busy eating to ask), shrimp and crab–all from right there in the lagoon. He explained that he was from the city of São Luís, on Brazil's northeastern coast, from whence came his penchant for sea food. To drink there was a heavenly concoction made of papaya.

"Let me see if I get this," Ray asked, between mouthfuls. "Santana sent his goon-squad to my place to kidnap us?"

"I doubt they would have gone through the trouble," Francesca corrected. "They would have probably just shot you on sight."

Ray swallowed. "And you know this because..."

"Because I overheard them at a little *soirée* he held on the his yacht a week ago. The occasion was the arrival of the "goon-squad" as you call it. Its real name is the Lightning Force, and man-for-man, it is probably the most highly trained, most effective military force in the world."

"Wait...what? I'm ex-military, and know a good deal about armies from around the world. How come I've never heard of these guys?"

"One of the things that makes them so effective is that very few people even know they exist. I had been married to Emídio several years before I knew they were anything more than his personal bodyguard. But they are much, much more than that. They are spread all over the world, and they are *not* to be trifled with."

She took a sip of papaya juice and continued. "Up until recently the only ones stationed on Cabrito were part of a special unit charged with guarding my husband. They wear a shield with a lightning bolt behind it, and I was fairly used to seeing them. I think James told me once he and Max's mother had a run-in with Conchita...she's in charge of that group. But now he has brought in a special group–a company, I think he called it–and they are officially in charge of the security of Cabrito. Even the Cabritan army answers to them. We had a little party to welcome the commanders of the group. They are led by a German named Friedrich Krugel. I remember a few of the lieutenants that were there that evening: a Frenchman named LaRue, another German named Stromm, and an Argentine (Ray thought he detected a scornful curl of her lip as she said this word) named Sanchez. I'm expected to show up at these things as 'eye candy'. After years of practice, I can play the part of the shallow supermodel very well, and they never suspect I have a brain." Here she smiled, if ever so slightly.

"While Emídio was off consulting with one of the commanders and the ever-present Conchita (there was that lip curl again), I overheard Larue speaking to Stromm in French about their mission. Because of my career in international fashion, I am fluent in several languages, a fact people tend to forget. I heard enough to realize that you, your daughter, and Max were in danger. From that point on I watched for signs of movement. Although to tell the truth, Inácio and Itamar finding you when they did was just plain lucky."

"If Max were here, he would say there was no such thing as luck," Cascavel piped up, his mouth still full of shrimp. "It was...." Suddenly conscious of whose presence he was in, he quickly chewed and swallowed. "It was God," he continued. Ray shot him a dirty look, partly for talking with his mouth full in front of the glamorous hostess, partly for inserting God into the discussion.

"We better hope there is some kind of divine intervention," said Francesca, "because as it stands, the devil is calling the shots."

Ray's eyebrows went up. "And by the devil you mean..."

"Emídio Santana, of course."

"How'd ya ever get saddled with a creep like that?" Ray wanted to know.

Francesca took another long sip on the papaya juice. "I met him during Rio Fashion Week in Brazil about ten years ago. He was tired of his first wife–an English duchess or something–and I was dazzled by his obvious wealth and power. After we married he brought me here, and I quickly realized I was nothing more than a trophy wife. He basically ignores me, and I've lost count of the affairs he has had over the years.

"The only good thing to come of this for me has been the island of Cabrito. I hate Emídio but I love this island."

"From what I can tell, the islanders are pretty fond of you as well." Ray noted.

Francesca smiled. "They are what keeps me here. I want to help them as much as I can–and for me that means working behind the scenes to undo some of the damage that Emídio and his father are doing."

"But we haven't seen George Santana around here in ages." observed Cascavel.

"He has come and gone a few times since I have lived here, but it's always very low-profile."

"Nobody needs to convince me that Santana is the devil impersonated," Ray said, "but what did you mean when you said he was calling the shots?"

"I mean that everything that is happening is on purpose and part of a big plan. I've heard Emídio refer to it often in conversations with his father and others. The details are sketchy, but whatever it is, it is going to be big. Much bigger than Cabrito."

"How does our little adventure at the airport fit in to the overall picture?" Cascavel asked.

"Like I said, the details have escaped me. However, you will be interested to know that shortly after that mishap at the airport, George Santana showed up and gave Emídio a tongue-lashing for not keeping on top of things here on the island. We were on the *Lua Negra*, and I could hear arguing from my personal suite midships."

Ray sat back and stroked his scraggly beard. "So based on what we know, George *and* Emídio are planning something big, but the success of their plan depends on the security of Cabrito. Max and Ilana's romp through the jungle threw a serious monkey-wrench into the system. So now they are tying up loose knots here. A *coup*, so to speak."

"Of sorts, although I doubt they'll get rid of *presidente* Ferraz just yet. I get the impression that he has been a very useful idiot over the years."

"Been there, done that," commented Ray, bitterly.

Cascavel put a reassuring hand on his shoulder. "*Senhor* Raimundo, we have all taken our turn dancing to the devil's tune. It's time to put all that behind us. Missionary Max says that God..."

"Ok, enough with the church service," Ray interrupted, irritation plainly evident in his voice. "We need to think about where we go from here."

"Well, based on what you have told me and what I have observed, you, your daughter, and Max are in serious trouble. We are going to need as many allies as we can get. The next step would seem to be to get in touch with Mr. Rockwell. I imagine he has already gotten in touch with his superiors at SPGI, and they are probably working on something."

"But we don't even know where he is."

Francesca held up her satellite phone. "I happen to have a number."

CHAPTER 11

WITH ENEMIES LIKE THESE...

The three Yamanis had been preparing a light breakfast when they suddenly found themselves surrounded by men dressed in black and toting assault rifles. The warriors had reached instinctively for their spears. Before Ilana could do or say anything all three of them were lying face down on the beach, the sand absorbing their blood.

"Don't shoot! Don't shoot! I'm an American!" Mary Sue screamed over and over as she crouched by the rocks, hands over her ears.

Ilana resisted the urge to grab one of the fallen warriors' spears and hurl it at these nameless, faceless assailants, but she knew she would never make it. With prodigious effort she subdued her emotions as she and Mary Sue were bound hand-and-foot and hoisted up the cliff. Knowing Max would be coming back shortly, she had managed to swing towards a jagged rock. The effort left her with a scratched leg, but it also left a shard of her *onça*-skin dress for Max to find later.

At the top their feet were unbound, and they were prodded into the dark forest. Ilana's jungle-trained eyes could tell they were following a trail of sorts, although to where she could not guess. She had adjusted mentally to their new situation and her mind was working in overdrive to come up with some sort of escape plan.

Esmeralda Island started life as a volcano. The cliffs surrounding the island rose to dizzying heights. Where they ended the jungle began, gently sloped uphill, crested, and then dipped back down. From the air the island looked like a large green bowl. By the time afternoon rolled around, Ilana surmised that they were nearing the bottom of the crater.

While Ilana was holding up with admirable courage, the same could not be said for Mary Sue. Her reactions swung from loud imprecatory proclamations of divine judgment to blubbering pleas for mercy. She alternately expressed indignation, prayed, and cried–all in an excruciatingly whiney voice.

This continued for over an hour until one of the armed men stuck the muzzle of his G36 in her face. "You shut up, or I kill you now," he hissed.

She shut up, and had Ilana's hands not been tied she might have hugged the man.

The rest of the trip was conducted in silence, until finally they reached what appeared to be a base camp. The captives were affixed firmly to trees. A muscular, olive-skinned man with jet black hair was obviously in charge. He gave orders for some of the men to eat, while others stood guard. Then, at his word, the guards came to eat while those who had just eaten assumed guard duty.

Ilana watched everything that went on. She observed the light of the sun through the trees, trying hard to get her bearings and an idea of the time.

One tree over, Mary Sue sobbed quietly.

After taking care of his men, the commander came over to inspect the prisoners. He examined them individually, then pointed to Mary Sue, barked an order, and turned walked across the camp to his tent. Two commandos immediately loosed Mary Sue from the tree, untied her feet, and guided her to their commander's quarters.

Max watched the whole scene, crouched in a thicket just outside the camp. Making good use of his special-forces training in the Brazilian rainforest, he had been able to catch up to the group shortly before they reached the base camp. He was positioned near the commander's tent, opposite where the captives were tied. As Mary Sue was taken into the commander's tent, Max began to formulate a plan.

If he could make his way around the perimeter of the camp, he could come up behind Ilana, unnoticed, and free her. Then, when they brought Mary Sue back, the two of them could overpower her guard before anybody could do anything about it and make their escape.

The plan had its weak points, Max knew. All it would take would be one sideways glance from one guard and every rifle barrel in the camp would be trained on him. Still, an imperfect plan was better than no plan at all.

He turned to make his way around the edge of the camp, and found himself face-to-face with twenty native warriors, all with arrows trained on him. Slowly he raised his hands, trying to remember some of the words he had learned in the Yamani tongue.

"Friend..." he managed to say, just before he felt the sharp blow to his head and was enveloped by darkness.

CHAPTER 12

THE ENEMY OF MY ENEMY...

President Osvaldo Ferraz seethed inwardly as the helicopter flew him back to the presidential mansion. For years he had endured the grating, patronizing manner of Emídio Santana. It was annoying, but Santana was his key to power–and once in power, was his key to staying there.

Back then the Santanas had only seemed interested in maintaining the *status quo*, and had interfered but little in the day-to-day affairs of the government. Among the heads of state of Latin and Central American banana republics, his had been a sweet gig.

Now, however, things were different. In the past month Santana had become much more "hands-on," and this was taking its toll on Ferraz's sanity. It was becoming increasingly clear to the current president of Cabrito that he was replaceable, just as the former president of Cabrito had been. In fact, if the current trends continued, such a replacement was becoming more and more likely.

President Ferraz was always in survival mode, but it was there, in the air somewhere between the Lua Negra and the *casa branca* that he went into *panicked* survival mode.

Borges, his portly chief of staff, met him at the landing pad. Ferraz told him to clear his schedule for the rest of the day. Then he went to his office and closed the tall rosewood doors behind him.

He had some thinking to do.

So engrossed in his thoughts was he that he didn't even pause to reflect at how small his desk was compared to the one on the *Lua Negra* when he sat down behind it. If he was going to take on the Santana cabal, it would take all the concentration he could muster.

And he would also need allies. His mind went down through a list of people who might hate Santana as much as he did. Surely the American missionary had no love for Emídio Santana, but then he was stranded somewhere on Esmeralda Island. The girl Ilana was already in Emídio's clutches, and, thanks in part to his own collusion, Santana was in complete control of SPGI.

The people's pharmacy! Ferraz gave a grim chuckle. *What a joke. The only thing it will ever cure will be the headache SPGI gave Santana and his family...*

Then a new question entered his mind: why had Emídio Santana insisted the SPGI be brought to the island in the first place? The invitation had been made by the Santana family, and subsequently rubber-stamped by the *presidente*. And now, a few short months later, it was commandeered, with Ferraz himself giving the "victory speech" for an event that he had virtually nothing to do with. Perhaps it had something to do with Santana's many references to "the final objective." Whatever that objective was, he was positive he wouldn't like it.

Suddenly Osvaldo Ferraz, head of the government of the Republic of Cabrito (in title if not in fact) felt very alone. All the things he enjoyed so much about his position–the trappings of power, the opulence, the people falling over themselves to carry out his wishes–all of this belonged to Santana and could be removed at will. He himself had nobody loyal to him, no one who would stick up for him in a conflict with Santana. That's why he would have to continue to suck up to the ingratiatingly patronizing scion of the leading family of Cabrito, and hope for the best.

Unless...

Unless there was someone who hated Santana as much or more than he did–someone powerful with whom he could join forces. And like a ray of light from above, Osvaldo Ferraz suddenly knew exactly who that person was.

Hands shaking, he picked up the phone to make the most important call of his life.

Lieutenant Sanchez regarded the trembling girl before him. In the years that had passed since he had been recruited out of the armed forces of his native Argentina to serve with the Lightning Force, he had participated in many interrogations. This one, he knew without a doubt, was going to be a cinch. Everyone else in this party had come prepared for the jungle–the other girl, the three Yamani, the man who had somehow eluded them–but this girl was completely out of place. What was she doing here? Whatever it was, she was obviously the weakest link in the chain, and thus the easiest to be broken.

He commanded the guard to untie the girl's wrists, then waved him away and motioned to a canvas chair. "Please," he said, "have a seat." The girl regarded him suspiciously for a moment, then sat down with obvious relief.

Sanchez got up and poured a cup of steaming hot coffee, then handed it to her. "It's Brazilian," he said, as she took it from his hand. "The Brazilians are inferior *futbol* players, but one has to admit, they make great coffee."

Sanchez waited patiently while the girl sipped at her coffee. He offered her a piece of bread with butter, which she accepted eagerly. After wolfing it down, she looked up at him curiously. "Who are you? Why did you kidnap us? Where is Max? What..." and with that she broke down into uncontrollable sobs.

Sanchez smiled and handed her a handkerchief. "There there, my dear. One thing at a time. I understand that you've had a rough day. You have many questions, and I have a few as well. But you must believe that I am your friend."

"W...who are you?"

"Ah, how rude of me. It is easy to forget one's manners in a wild place such as this." He waved his hands indicating the jungle outside. "My name is Pablo Sanchez, and I'm the one in charge of this little unit. My job is to maintain peace and order here in the jungle."

Mary Sue stopped sobbing and looked up at him. "You mean you're like... forest rangers?"

"Yes... forest rangers." Sanchez flashed her his warmest smile. "And I must apologize for the way you were brought here. My men believed you were part of the group of troublemakers they apprehended, but it is quite obvious to me that you do not belong with them. And that brings me to a question I have: what is a nice girl like you doing with a group of criminals like that?"

Mary Sue was confused. "Criminals?"

"Yes, indeed. But forgive me, perhaps you didn't know that the savages you are traveling with were a group of renegades who constantly stir up trouble with the other tribes."

"But... but they *shot* them!"

"That was regrettable, but my men assure me that it was a matter of self-defense. Did they or did they not go for their weapons?"

"They did..." Mary Sue admitted, "But what about Ilana?"

"Ah, Ilana. Educated in the finest schools on Cabrito, at government expense. Sent to the university in the US, also at the expense of the Cabritan government. And now, she works with a foreign company to undermine that very government. I don't get mixed up in the politics on Cabrito, but still... it would seem she is a tad ungrateful, wouldn't you say?"

Mary Sue felt a small surge of triumph. She *knew* that Ilana girl was trouble. What kind of mess had she gotten Max into? Well she, Mary Sue, was going to get Max *out* of that mess. And when this whole thing was over they would both go back to Greensborough and to the way things were before.

"I knew they were up to no good!" she exclaimed. "The only reason I came was to make sure Max didn't do anything that would get him hurt."

Sanchez' ears perked up. "You're a very brave girl...I'm sorry, I didn't get your name."

"Mary Sue."

"Well, Mary Sue, this Max fellow is certainly lucky to have a woman like you looking after him. Of course, as...er...forest rangers it is our job to make sure that innocent civilians don't come to any harm. Can you tell us where he is?"

"No, he went out to try to find a way up the cliff, just before you captured us...I mean, rescued me. I hope he's okay..." And with that she teared up again.

The lieutenant offered another handkerchief, which was gratefully accepted. "Now then, we need to find this Max as soon as possible, before he...before anything bad happens to him. Is there anything you can tell us?"

Mary Sue sniffed. "He...he used to be in the Army. He hasn't told me a lot, but I think he used to be very dangerous before... before he settled down."

Sanchez lifted his own cup of coffee in a salute. "But of course, the beauty has tamed the beast!"

Mary Sue found herself liking Sanchez a lot. He was courteous and well spoken, and he oozed sincerity. He had not spoken sharply to her at all, which was more than she could say for her boyfriend. Certainly Max could learn something from Lieutenant Sanchez in the manners department.

"Now my dear," Sanchez was saying, "you are free to go. Of course you can't go very far in this jungle, but you may walk about the camp as you like. I will have my men reserve one of the tents for you. They will be preparing lunch in about an hour, and you are free to join them. I just ask that you not associate with the other prisoner."

"Oh, no problem. I don't want anything more to do with *her*. I do hope you find Max soon."

"So do I, my dear, so do I." With that, Sanchez waved a hand, dismissing her.

Outside Ilana saw Mary Sue come out of the tent, alone. She tried to get her attention with her eyes, but the American girl ignored her completely. Instead, she walked over to where three soldiers were nursing a fire to life. She sat on a rock and watched as they worked, talking to them occasionally.

What is she doing? Ilana wondered. Curious, she turned her thoughts back to her escape plan.

Francesca put the phone down. Her expression was solemn as she turned to Ray and Cascavel. "We won't be getting any help from Regina Sherman anytime soon."

Briefly she summarized her conversation with James Rockwell. "James has been ordered by the government to leave the country on the next flight. Regina asked him to stay, and he is going to try, but it will involve him going underground for a while."

"That pasty-white bald guy? Hiding here in Cabrito?" Ray was doubtful. "He'll stick out like...like Pavarotti at the Grand Ole Opry."

That the comparison was lost on every single one of his listeners didn't seem to faze Ray one bit.

"My experience with Mr. Rockwell tells me he is very resourceful," replied Francesca. "I wouldn't bet against him. Still, while he *is* an ally, he can be of no help to us right now."

"So what can we do?" Ray wanted to know. "We can't just sit here."

"We can pray," piped up Cascavel. "Just like Max and Ilana did that day in the jungle. Then you showed up!"

Ray sighed. "The problem is, I'm here, and I don't have my plane, or my house, or anything. We are stuck. We..."

He looked around to see Cascavel sitting, head bowed, lips moving. He turned back to his hostess. "Francesca, I..." But she was also seated, her bowed head resting on her hand, her mouth moving in fervent intercession. "The whole world's gone batty," Ray grumbled and went outside for some fresh air.

Still muttering under his breath, Ray walked down the gangplank of the little cottage. Just as he set his foot onto the pristine beach a rustling noise caught his attention. Looking up he saw five soldiers in Cabritan uniforms emerge from the jungle, rifles at the ready.

CHAPTER 13

NO SACRIFICE TOO GREAT

The first thing Max noticed was the dull ache in his head, accompanied by an incessant pounding. He was lying on his back, and whatever he was lying on was not comfortable. He tried to move, but couldn't seem to get his arms or legs to cooperate.

Slowly he opened his eyes. The light assaulted him, and he closed them again, quickly. The pounding in his head was surprisingly rhythmic. Opening his eyes again, he found himself looking at the open sky. Turning his head slowly to the side and squinting, he saw that the pounding was far more than a sensation in his head: it emanated from dozens of drums being beaten by feather-plumed warriors.

As his eyes began to focus, he saw that he was in a sort of courtyard, bordered by a low stone wall. Turning his head the other direction he saw that he was at lying at the foot of a pyramid-shaped tower with a stone staircase running up the middle. The tower was built into the side of a cliff, which itself formed part of the volcanic wall that surrounded the center of the island. At the top of the tower a gaping hole led straight into the cliff. To Max it looked like someone had transplanted a temple from one of the Aztec ruins and inserted it into the rock face of the cliff, leaving only the front half visible. There were openings in the rock wall on either side of the temple and Max could only guess at the labyrinth of tunnels that ran back behind it. It wasn't hard to imagine that one of them led back to the arrow-filled skeletons he had seen earlier.

Max's still-groggy brain recognized the genius of the city's location. The tower commanded a view of most of the volcanic basin, leaving an enemy no choice but to try to approach it from behind. Yet the rock face actually leaned forward and overshadowed the apex of the tower, making it impossible to reach from above. Max imagined that the whole city could take refuge in the tunnels, and, with innumerable openings around the island, surprise counter-attacks could be mounted from any point, at any time. The outcropping would also have the effect–unforeseen by the original builders–of shielding the structure from the view of airplanes and satellite cameras.

There was no doubt in Max's mind that he had been brought to Icxi Xahn, the ancient sacred city of the Yamani and current home of the Shadow People.

Except the people around him were no shadows. With some effort, Max turned his head back towards the drummers. They stood in a semi-circle around him, festooned with bright feathers and beating out in unison their slow, throbbing, hypnotic rhythm. Behind them, Max could see that the courtyard was filled with people. Men, women and children–it seemed the whole city of Icxi Xahn had turned out for his this spectacle.

From what he could tell, Max was on a raised dais, lying on a pile of furs. His hands and feet were tightly bound. He was in the process of trying to figure out if there was any slack to the ropes when a shadow fell over him. He looked up and saw three figures–two of them very familiar. The dull roar of the crowd died down immediately upon their arrival.

"I hope you are enjoying your stay on Esmeralda Island." The oily voice could belong to none other than Diego, the prison guard turned lackey of Emídio Santana. Cascavel, who had spent more than his share of time in prison, once told Max that guards and prisoners alike referred to Diego as *o Diabo*–the Devil. Certainly this name had not been given to him for his pleasant disposition.

Max had last seen Diego on the tarmac of the Santo Expedito International Airport. Diego had been preparing to shoot Max– and would probably have succeeded had not a distraught Cascavel hit him with a flying tackle.

As Max lay there, he noticed that Diego looked a little worse for wear. His once pristine army uniform now had a rather bedrag- gled aspect. His face, which usually sported a thin, well-trimmed mustache, now featured a scraggly five o'clock shadow. And those small, cruel black eyes had taken on a wild–some would say cra- zy–look.

To Diego's right stood another familiar figure–this one as ro- tund as Diego was thin. It was Owanalehe, the corpulent witch doctor who, at Diego's urging, had instigated the entire Yamani gathering to try to make Max and Ilana their midnight snack. When he saw Max looking at him now, Owanalehe gave a broad smile revealing several spaces where teeth should have been. Ob- viously he was relishing Max's current predicament.

To Diego's left stood someone Max had never seen before. Had it not been for her feathery native gown–which she wore with re- gal aplomb–the young woman before him would have been totally out of place in that setting. Her skin was fair, her eyes bright green. Her face had a generous smattering of freckles and her hair was a flaming red that made Max's own carrot-top seem dull brown by comparison. And despite whatever pretenses the other two might have, she was obviously the one in charge.

She stood there, ramrod straight, eyeing Max with an aloof sort of curiosity. Diego was speaking again:

"You are in Icxi Xahn, my friend. It's an amazing place, really. The People of the Shadows came here to escape the wars of the Ya- mani, and set up housekeeping where their ancestors had left off millennia ago. It's fascinating, and I would give you a guided tour, but I'm afraid there won't be time for that. You see, in just a few hours, you, Missionary Max, are going to participate in a different kind of religious service. Don't worry, no need to prepare a homily. Oh no, you're not going to be behind the altar. You're going to be *on* it." Clearly pleased with his little speech, he swept his hand dramatically towards the apex of the pyramid, where a stone altar was visible.

Max knew that showing fear here would be just what Diego wanted. So instead he gave him a warm smile, ignoring the pain of the ropes cutting into his wrists and ankles. "Diego, or should I say *Diabo*, always a pleasure! I haven't seen you since...let's see...I think it was back there on the runway, wasn't it?"

Diego smiled thinly at this reference to their last meeting. Then he turned and said something to the woman beside him. Max didn't understand it, but whatever he said, it had its desired effect. Her expression changed to one of righteous indignation. With quick, determined steps she strode over to him, balled her hand into a fist, brought her arm back, and punched him right between the eyes.

Just before the darkness overtook him once again, he noticed a heart-shaped gold pendant swinging from her neck, with the word "Amanda" engraved across the front.

Regina Sherman found the Greensborough Construction Company with no problem, though, arriving as she did as dusk was setting in, the gates were closed and padlocked.

Not to be deterred, she remembered that Max had "gotten religion" while living in the small upstate town. With that in mind, she began to cruise the snowy streets, looking for churches. Her GPS showed an avenue marked "Church Street". She figured that would be a good place to start, and as she turned the corner, she saw she was right. Five grand old stone churches lined one side of the road.

Her first stop was at the large Catholic church–by far the grandest and the oldest in the line. The priest there professed no knowledge of a Maxwell Sherman, but asked if she would like to take confession while she was there. She mumbled something about having thoughts of murder, and went back out to her car.

The Methodist and Episcopalian churches were empty. She opened the door of the Unitarian church only to see a group of middle-aged women sitting around a candle and intoning some monosyllabic chant. She couldn't begin to imagine her Max involved in anything even remotely resembling that, so she turned around and quietly closed the door behind her.

The Baptist minister regretfully informed her that he too had no knowledge of Max, but then, just as Regina was about to return to her car, he stopped her.

"There's another church on the outskirts of town. It's an old white clapboard building. The pastor is a friend of mine, and he really seems to click with the younger guys. Perhaps you should try there."

Regina thanked him, got directions, went back to the Bentley. As she pulled onto the road the snow ban to fall more thickly, and in large, wet flakes. Ignoring the weather conditions, she gunned the motor and pulled out onto the road.

As she approached the perimeter of the little town, the houses and business establishments began to thin out–being replaced by little dairy farms, their pastures and cornfields covered with an ever increasing layer of white.

Looking at her GPS, Regina saw she was almost at the place where the Baptist minister had told her to make a left turn. When she looked back in front of her she had to stomp on the brake hard in order not to hit the cow standing directly in her path.

The tires of the British luxury vehicle spun as if desperately searching for a foothold on the icy pavement. The car twirled around two or three times before plowing into a snow bank.

Heart pounding, fingers white against the steering while, Regina sat there, stunned. The motor had stalled, so she turned the key in the ignition and was relieved when it roared to life. But getting out of the snow bank was not going to be so easy. She put the car in reverse and gunned it, but the more the wheels spun, the deeper she sunk into the fluffy white snow. After about five minutes of trying, she gave up.

For the first time since she could remember, Regina Sherman was completely helpless. Her cell phone sat on the seat beside her, but who could she call? All the people who were usually at her beck and call–falling over themselves to do her bidding–now worked for someone else, someone who would have no inclination whatsoever to help her. In fact, she imagined that George Santana would get a perverse satisfaction were he to learn of her predicament.

And she knew nobody in this town. All her planning, all her strategizing, all her cool calculations...all for naught. Regina placed her head in her hands and, for the first time in years–indeed, for the first time since the death of her husband–she cried.

She cried, and then she prayed. She had no idea who she was talking to, or how to go about it. She simply cried out in agony and despair.

"God, whoever you are, wherever you are...help me!"

There were other words that got lost in the sobs, but they all held the same sense of utter helplessness.

A sharp rap on her window interrupted her prayers. She looked up to see a youngish man peering in at her. He wore a green winter cap, and a friendly smile. She lowered the window.

"Looks like you could use some help, ma'am."

"Yes...please..." was all she could manage. He couldn't help but notice the streaks on her face left by the tears.

"Well, you just wait right there, and I'll have you pulled out in a jiffy." He motioned behind him to his Ford pickup truck. "Then you can come over to the house and my wife, Anne, will fix you up a nice cup of hot chocolate."

"Thanks," she replied simply. Then, "My name is Regina."

The man smiled even more broadly and stuck a gloved hand through the window. "Howdy! Folks around here call me Pastor Dave."

CHAPTER 14

FRESH ALTAR NATIVES

ay realized that trying to get back to the cottage would be useless. The armed men in front of him could cut him to ribbons the moment he turned around. Silently he cursed himself for his carelessness, then, slowly, he raised his hands into the air.

"*Seu* Raimundo, where are the others?"

Ray did a double take. The soldier standing closest to him was grinning, and his rifle was at rest. Then he looked closer, and began to grin as well. The man standing before him was Lúcio, one of the men in Max's martial arts group. Upon further examination he saw that the other four were also part of the group, as well as regular attenders at the Peace Church.

"What are you guys doing here?"

"Bernardinho called us yesterday to say that Max had gone to Esmeralda Island for some reason. Then Sebastião here saw you and Cascavel heading up into the jungle with a couple strange guys in the back seat. So we borrowed a jeep and decided to investigate. We found the VW pulled over on the side of the road, and followed the trail down to here. We were..."

Lúcio stopped talking suddenly and all five men brought their rifles up. Ray looked behind him to see that Itamar and Inácio had stepped out onto the walkway, Uzis at the ready.

"Oh, hey, guys...calm down!" exclaimed Ray. He introduced the two bodyguards. When he mentioned whose bodyguards they were, the soldiers' eyes grew wide. "You mean..."

"Yep. Francesca Santana is one of the good guys...er...gals." At about that time Francesca came outside, followed closely by Cascavel. When the soldiers saw her they removed their hats. While Cabritans' attitudes toward Emídio Santana ranged from ambivalence to downright hostility, they revered his Brazilian wife. It was common to hear people comment on how unfortunate she had been in her choice of a husband.

"Yes," someone would inevitably reply, "but it worked out well for Cabrito."

Besides her stunning beauty and international recognition in the fashion industry–both of which were sources of pride to the Cabritans–there was her Brazilian nationality. Most of Cabrito's limited TV programming came from Brazil, and when World Cup time rolled around most young men could be seen sporting the blue and yellow jersey of the *Seleção Brasileira*. Thus, because of her origins in the interior of Minas Gerais, Francesca was an automatic celebrity.

But what endeared her most to the Cabritans was the fact that she very obviously loved their island, their culture...*them*. Her involvement in social work was legendary. Schools, hospitals, urban projects–all had been recipients of her generosity.

Emídio encouraged this, as it could only help his standing in the community. But the Cabritans knew that the source of these improvements in their lives was Francesca, and not her jet-setting, *mulherengo* husband.

Francesca swung the door open and motioned for them to come in, which they did–trooping up the gangplank and looking at her sheepishly as they passed.

Once inside she had Inácio whip up some lunch for them. As they were eagerly wolfing it down, Cascavel came up beside Ray, an impish grin on his face.

"You see, *meu amigo*, answers to prayer don't always have to come in the form of an old guy flying over the jungle in an airplane left over from World War One."

"It's from World War Two, and just leave it alone, will you?" Ray grumbled back.

After the men had eaten their late lunch, they all gathered in the living room and got down to the business at hand. The soldiers told of the general order that had gone out to be on the lookout for Max, Ray, and Ilana. They also told of the Lightning Force, and how many in the Cabritan army were resentful of what they perceived to be a foreign intrusion on their soil.

After catching everybody up on the situation, Ray sat back and stroked his chin thoughtfully. "It seems to me," he said finally, "that we have two big problems. One: we have no idea what Santana's big plan is. If we knew what was after, we could get a step or two ahead of him. Two: Max and Ilana are on Esmeralda Island."

Suddenly, Fancesca's satellite phone rang. She picked it up, then excused herself and went out to the veranda. Her guests could hear her talking in serious tones, but could not make out the gist of the conversation. When she returned about ten minutes later her face beamed.

"Gentlemen," she pronounced, "We have a plan, and a surprising new ally."

The first red streaks of sunset were visible in the sky, but Max was less than appreciative of their beauty. His hands were still tightly bound behind his back, and he was on his feet, being prodded up the stone steps of the pyramid temple by the tips of native spears. At the apex of the stairway stood Diego, Owanalehe, and the mysterious red-headed woman. Below him the drums continued their incessant rhythm

As he ascended the staircase, Max looked around him. Below was a sea of humanity, jumping, pumping their fists, screaming for blood. Raising his eyes, Max saw city of Icxi Xahn, stretching out on all sides from the temple. Parts of it appeared to be well used, while other parts looked like they had never been reclaimed from the jungle. The stone buildings gradually gave way to the lush green jungle, which in turn gently sloped upward as it followed the ridge that formed a ring around the city. Under normal circumstances he would have loved to explore every nook and cranny of the ancient city. As it was, there were more pressing matters at hand.

Arriving at the top of the stone temple, Max faced his foes. Diego wore an expression of venomous triumph, while Owanalehe simply grinned his ubiquitous, dentally-challenged grin. Max decided that any appeal to either of these monsters would be a waste of effort.

Acting on a desperate hunch, he turned to the regal-looking red-head and looked her straight in the eyes. "Hello, Amanda," he said in English.

The woman cocked her head to one side. Diego motioned to two warriors, and they grabbed Max roughly by the arms.

"Amanda?" he repeated. She looked at him harder now. Was it his imagination, or was she mouthing the word *Amanda*?

As the soldiers began to drag him toward the altar Max racked his brain for Yamani words, then asked "Is your name 'Amanda'?"

"Shut up!" Diego stepped forward and slapped him across the face.

Max's mind raced back a couple weeks. He and Ilana were in the old marketplace of Santo Expedito, where Max was trying to find a suitable gift for Mary Sue. A pretty necklace caught his eye. Ilana noticed him looking at it.

"Lhamhoqua" she said.

"What?"

"Lhamhoqua. It's necklace, in Yamani."

And Max had remembered it because it sounded so much like "Lamoka", the name of a lake in the Fingler Lakes region of New York where his father had taken him fishing once as a boy.

"Amanda...*lhamhoqua!*" he fairly shouted in Yamani as the warriors lifted him, squirming, onto the altar. He wondered if he had gotten the word right, and then saw her look down and take the gold pendant in her hands. Diego was livid. Owanalehe had stopped grinning. He pulled a wicked looking knife from his waistband and raised up over Max.

"Amanda...*lahmhoqua!*" Max gave one last effort as the knife descended.

"STOP!" The command was in Yamani, and came from the red-headed woman, who simultaneously stepped forward and grabbed the witch-doctor's knife-arm, stopping it in mid descent. Max breathed a sigh of relief.

Then ensued an animated conversation between the three. Max couldn't understand much of what was being said, but he noted that the two men were increasingly put out, while the woman was stubbornly adamant. She stood there with her arms crossed, glowering at the men as they argued with her. Every once in a while she would stomp her foot in determination and say something, which resulted in more aggravation on the part of Diego and Owanalehe.

Finally the woman turned to the warriors and barked an order. Immediately they reached down and lifted him from the altar. Not bothering to untie him–or even set him down–they carried him back down the stairway, followed closely by the red-headed queen. The drums paused in their beating, and the gathered multitude craned their necks, wondering why the ceremony had been interrupted.

Diego threw his cap to the ground and spewed a string of the most potent curses in the arsenal of the Portuguese language. Owanalehe stood with his lips pursed, watching them descend.

It took great effort on the part of three burly men to get a loudly protesting Ilana into the commander's tent. Once she was there, bound tightly to a chair, the climate was openly hostile on both sides. Unlike the interview Sanchez had conducted with Mary Sue, there were no pleasantries, no courteous speech, and certainly no coffee. From her seat by the fire outside the tent, Mary Sue could hear most of the conversation. She didn't need to understand Portuguese to get the gist of the angry questions posed by Sanchez, and the defiant non-answers and imprecatory accusations proffered by Ilana in return.

She felt a slight twinge of guilt at leaving Max's friend to such a fate while she sat warmly but the fire. But then she rationalized that it was this woman, this uncivilized savage called Ilana, that had gotten Max mixed up in this sordid affair in the first place.

And besides, these men were obviously authorities–and didn't the Bible say to obey authorities? She would have to remember to have a talk about that with Max when this was all over.

After about half an hour the guards brought a still-defiant Ilana out of the tent and returned her to her tree. Slowly the camp fires began to dim and flicker. Mary Sue wrapped herself in a blanket that had been provided for her, made herself as comfortable as possible, and soon fell into a deep, dreamless sleep.

CHAPTER 15

A RAY OF LIGHT

"You better have a pretty good reason for coming here at this hour, uninvited," Santana growled.

"You mean besides the fact that I am president of Cabrito?" Ferraz replied cooly as he stepped off the helipad onto the deck of the luxury yacht. Behind him the blades of the presidential helicopter gave a few final turns before coming to rest.

Santana met this impertinence with a stony glare, matched by the expression on the ever-present Conchita's face. Ferraz was getting uppity of late, and would have to be dealt with. All in good time...

"It just so happens that I have some matters of importance to discuss with you. Matters having to do with your plans... *Very* important matters. Though the Santana family is very influential here in Cabrito, I am still commander and chief of the armed forces. And the armed forces are not at all content with recent events. If things are allowed to continue as they are, we may have a full-blown military coup on our hands."

"Osvaldo Ferraz, are you threatening me?"

"Not at all," replied the *presidente* mildly. "Of course these developments distress me greatly, and I will do everything in my power to bring our troops into line. But for me to do that, I have to know what your...what *our* objectives are."

Santana glowered at Ferraz for a few seconds, and the *presidente* held his breath. Finally the taller man sighed and shrugged his shoulders. "Come on then."

Ferraz breathed a sigh of relief as they made their way toward the main quarters. He had taken a gamble, he knew, but the veiled threat of a civil war gave him an ever-so-slight leverage point. Santana was not ready to take on the entire Cabritan military establishment... not yet.

Santana was just reaching for the door when the sound of another helicopter disrupted the peaceful night air. All three looked up to see the chopper–smaller than the one already resting on deck–make its descent. It landed gracefully on the adjacent deck and the pilot cut the engine.

The door opened upward with a hiss of the hydraulic arm, and Santana groaned audibly. Out stepped Francesca Santana, followed by an orderly towing her suitcase. She strode purposefully across the deck, here face set, eyes blazing with fury. The orderly stood behind her, head bowed in deference.

"Emídio Santana! If you think you can simply spend your days playing like an oversized adolescent out here on this glorified bath toy and leave your own wife to gather dust back at that drafty old firetrap you call a mansion, you must be insane!"

Santana's mouth was open, but no words came out. Ferraz and Conchita exchanged surprised glances. "But *querida, I...*"

"Don't you *querida* me, you filthy old man. I am sick and tired of being left by myself in that dump. I'm not going to stay there one more minute."

"But *queri...* Francesca. I'm very busy..."

"I don't care one bit how 'busy' you are. You just go on doing whatever it is you do, and playing with your little friends (here she cast a disdainful look at Conchita). I'm going to make myself comfortable here on the yacht. God knows this tub is big enough,

I should be able to spend days out here without ever seeing your wretched face. Come, Sérgio."

And with that she stormed off towards the guest quarters followed by Sérgio, the wheels of her little suitcase clicking behind her. Ferraz, Santana, and Conchita stared after her in stunned silence.

Finally Ferraz chuckled, breaking the spell. "Brazilian women! They certainly are firecrackers." Santana grunted and opened the door. The two men walked through, but Conchita held back.

"Aren't you coming?" Santana asked.

"I'll be there in a minute." she replied. "I need to check on something." Again Santana shrugged and the two men entered the cabin. Before the door closed behind them President Ferraz glanced back worriedly at Conchita, who was striding purposefully across the deck.

Raymond Sand cursed as he maneuvered his rickety VW back down the mountain trail it had climbed earlier in the day. The rough trail and treacherous curves were made more dangerous by the fact that it was night. The only light came from his own headlights; the rest was pitch black. His mind raced over the events of the last forty-eight hours. His daughter was on Esmeralda Island, meeting with who knew what kind of danger, and he had no way of communicating with her, no way of protecting her. It was some comfort to know that Max was there, but not much. He would have greatly preferred to be there himself.

The plan they had concocted with Francesca looked good on paper, but there were all kinds of things that could go wrong. His part of it was to meet up with Mr. Rockwell. Together they would try to re-establish contact with Max and inform him of the developments with SPGI. For this reason he was on his way back to Santo Expedito, with directions to the place the fugitive businessman was hiding out.

It seemed solid, but Ray couldn't escape that overwhelming feeling that things were spinning out of control. As the lights of Santo Expedito came into view between the trees he reached over to the glove compartment, removed a small flask, and began to undo the metal cap. He could already anticipate the feeling the warm liquid would give as it went down his throat and then set fire to his brain.

He held the bottle in his hand and sloshed the tantalizing drink around a few times. He reflected on how he had always scoffed at Max for being weak, for having to rely on an invisible, imaginary God in times of trouble. But *this*, this fiery concoction in a bottle, this was his god. He turned to it when life got complicated, and relied on it to bring him through. And what did he get in return? Impaired judgement, destroyed relationships, cotton-mouth, and killer hangovers.

And inexplicably, for the first time, Ray began to contrast that with what he saw in Max and Ilana–a faith that not only saw them through the rough times, but allowed them to maintain their lucidity...their dignity.

Unbidden, long-repressed memories began to play in his head. Memories of a white clapboard church in North Dakota, of happy faces gathered on Sunday, of men behind the pulpit opening the Bible and proclaiming the Gospel in urgent tones.

Then the memories turned ugly. They focused on his own laughing rejection of all he had known, his gradual descent into the hell of alcoholism. The military had provided him with a safe haven, and he had excelled there–but weekend passes were marked by drunken parties that let him know he was still mastered by the bottle. All his attempts at self reformation had been completely useless, and he had come to believe that the way things were was the way things ought to be.

At that moment the bottle in his hand lost all attraction for Ray. The liquid inside no longer sparkled like gold. Indeed, to Ray it bore an uncanny resemblance to the gutter water that ran in the less-developed neighborhoods of Santo Expedito. On an impulse, he rolled down the window and hurled the bottle out into the darkness. And as he heard it shatter he felt a freedom like he had never felt before.

He stopped the car and bowed his head. "Lord," he began, his voice gruff with emotion. "I ain't talked to you much in a long time. All these years I've been tryin' to handle things on my own. And I just keep getting myself deeper and deeper into trouble. Well, you brought Max into my life, and then Ilana... and I think I finally understand that I can't do it by myself. I remember Max telling me once that that's the point... that it's not what I do, but what Jesus did two-thousand years ago. So, I tell you right now–I believe. I believe in Jesus, I believe in what He did, and I believe He's the only way–just like Max keeps telling me."

And at that moment the car flooded with light.

So great was Ray's feeling of relief after the great struggle of his soul had ended, that for a moment he thought he was being bathed in a divine beam straight from heaven.

"Thank-you Lord," he breathed.

Then he heard the voice. "Please step out of the car."

"Lord?"

Turning around, he saw that the source of the illumination: the spotlight from a Land Rover.

"*Senhor* Raymond Sand, please step out of the car."

This is a bit of overkill for just throwing a bottle out the window. Ray mumbled as he opened the door. *Since when have the police started enforcing litter laws?* And as he stepped out onto the road and stood up facing the light, it dawned on him that, as far as he knew, the police on Cabrito did not use Land Rovers.

Suddenly his mind snapped into gear and he jerked back in an attempt to get back into his car, and that movement caused the bullet to hit his shoulder, not his heart.

The impact spun him around. He bounced off the front of the Beetle and hit the ground. As he tried to rise again another bullet slammed into his leg. He dropped to the ground and didn't move, hoping against hope that the shooters would leave him for dead.

Footsteps approached and he heard voices.

"I think he's dead."

"Better make sure. Put a bullet in his head."

"Yes sir!"

Ray clenched his teeth, expecting any minute to be dispatched to his eternal reward. And, through the fog of pain, he remembered a message he had heard back in that old midwestern white clapboard church. It was the story of Christ on the cross, talking to the thief crucified next to him. And the words "This day you will be with me in paradise" burned their way into his consciousness and brought a strange, other-worldly comfort to his soul.

Then there was a gunshot, and Ray lay still.

CHAPTER 16

SURVIVAL SKILLS

Ray felt the bullet burn the back of his head. He blacked out... and then regained consciousness a moment later. Something warm was running down the back of his neck. In the distance he heard the armored car gear up and leave. He opened his eyes slightly. Everything was dark. He remained still, lying in the dirt, half under his car, for what seemed like hours.

Finally, satisfied that nobody was around, he reached with his good arm and felt the back of his head. Amazingly, the bullet had just grazed him. The ground around his head was damp with blood.

Forcing his muscles to move, he crawled slowly towards the still-open door of the old VW. With every ounce of strength he had he pulled himself into the driver's seat. His head was swimming, but he knew that if he wanted to survive, he had to drive. The key was in the ignition, and he turned it. The VW coughed to life, and Ray breathed a prayer of thanksgiving and began his painful descent towards Santo Expedito.

Night had fallen over Esmeralda Island, and Tanawehe, revered queen of the People of the Shadows, sat on her throne in the royal palace in Icxi Xahn and glowered at the two men before her. Feather-clad guards stood at all three entranceways, and torches flickered from the walls. The mood was tense, to say the least.

Two weeks earlier the fat witch doctor and the strange white man had appeared in Icxi Xahn, warning of an impending attack on their city by their Yamani brethren. She had been surprised to learn of the existence of the other Yamani, because the firm belief for centuries had been that the warring tribes on the main island had killed themselves off. The counsel of these newcomers had been to make a pre-emptive attack–counsel which Tanawehe had been reluctant to accept at first. Finally convinced of the wisdom of such a move, they made their preparations, crossed the watery span between their island and the main island, and attacked without warning. Tanawehe herself had led them.

They had achieved utter surprise, catching their erstwhile enemies completely off guard. While her warriors–and the two visitors–had been exultant, Tanawehe had noticed no preparations for war in the villages they had raided. How could villages planning an attack be so completely unprepared?

Then the white soldiers had appeared in her jungle. The pasty one–called Diego–had assured her that they were her friends, and had come to help in the event of possible retaliation against the Shadow People. Reluctantly, Tanawehe allowed them to stay. She even sent her own warriors out to make sure these new friends–so obviously unused to the ways of the jungle–remained unharmed.

And then the patrol had brought back this man. According to their report, he was different from the other white men. He moved through the jungle as if he had been there before. And he was obviously hostile to their new friends, spying on them, seeking to free their prisoners.

Oh yes, the prisoners! Two women, one Yamani and one not. Diego and the fat shaman had assured her that these interlopers were part of the plot on the part of their Yamani brethren to destroy them–witches sent to weave a powerful and malignant curse. But, if they were so powerful, why had they been captured so easily?

Despite these misgivings, and at the insistence of the witch doctor and her own priests, she had ordered the sacrifice of the white man–even though she wished to know more about him. Diego had told her what he said when he had regained consciousness there in the courtyard, how he had insulted their gods and besmirched her honor. Outraged, she had knocked him out again.

Then, just as he was about to be dispatched to the gods, he had looked her in the eyes and said that word: *Amanda.* And something...she couldn't say what...stirred deep within her. The fact that he had looked at her golden necklace, the one everyone said was a gift from the gods, had made her even more curious.

So now she needed answers, and the two men standing before her were not giving them to her.

"Majesty," the pasty one was saying, "you cannot possibly know what danger you have put yourself in by leaving this man alive."

"Are you suggesting," she replied, disdain dripping from her lips, "that Tanawehe, queen of the People of the Shadows, daughter of Tan, the god of Thunder, is incapable of taking care of herself?"

Diego opened his mouth to answer, then stopped. He looked at his companion for help. The fat witch doctor just stood there and grinned his stupid, toothless grin.

After a moment of awkward silence Tanawehe stood and drew herself up majestically. She stood close to six feet, and the plumage she wore as a headdress made her seem all the more imposing. Her flashing eyes bored into the two men before her, who suddenly felt very small. "You tell me this man is dangerous to me...to my people. Yet you do not tell me why, exactly. You cannot answer why he used that word...*Amanda*...or what it is supposed to mean.

"You sent my people to battle, claiming that our long-forgotten brethren were planning war against us. Yet, when we arrived, we found no evidence of such plans. There were no painted warriors, no sharpened spears, no strung bows. To the contrary, we found people peacefully asleep in their dwellings. Centuries ago we came to the this island for peace. Now you have brought war upon us again."

Diego started to say something but the queen held up her hand, and he snapped his mouth shut.

"*Your* warriors are traipsing through our jungle, scaring off the game we depend on for food, claiming to protect us. And still we do not know from what or from whom. You are full of words, but you have no answers."

"But majesty..." Diego broke in weakly, not really sure what he was going to say, but at the same time not liking at all the way the conversation was headed.

"Silence!" Diego closed his mouth.

"Well now I will get some answers," the queen continued. "You both will remain here under guard, while I go talk to the man you almost killed. Perhaps he will be honest with Tanawehe. If not, Tanawehe will know." She made this last declaration while fingering a long knife she wore at her waist. The implication–that it would be employed on whoever was lying to her–was not lost on the hearers.

With that she stepped down off the dais and strode out of the throne room, motioning for one of her guards to follow her. By the door she paused long enough to take a torch down from the wall, then left, guard in tow. Diego and the witch doctor looked at each other, then at the guards that surrounded them. Things were not going according to plan, and each was sure the other was to blame.

When the VW engine coughed to life, Ray could not know that his assailants were only about half a kilometer up the trail–within easy earshot. Looking at each other incredulously, they wheeled the Land Rover around to give chase. Ray had been driving for just a few minutes when they caught up to him. Bright light again illuminated the car. Ray pressed his foot to the pedal, just as a hail of bullets pierced his car, shattering the windows and lodging themselves in the dashboard. Ray felt another sharp pain in his right arm.

*There's only one way...*he realized, and gritted his teeth. Hands gripping the steering wheel, he made a sharp, right-hand turn without slowing down in the least. The VW broke through some underbrush, ran up a rock ledge, and flew out into the blackness– wheels spinning, engine screaming.

Back on the road, the armored car slowed to a stop. The soldiers descended from their vehicle and looked down into the yawning abyss. There were no sounds, no lights, no sign of life.

"There is no way anybody could have survived that," said one of the men.

"Agreed," affirmed the leader. He pulled out his two-way. "Lieutenant LaRue to base," he began in his thick French accent. "Target two eliminated. Raymond Sand has, as the English say, cashed in *ze* chimps. Break."

CHAPTER 17

ULTERIOR MOTIVES

Francesca opened the door to a spacious cabin on the first floor below the main deck of the *Lua Negra* and motioned for her orderly to enter. Then she closed the door behind them.

"Quickly, Cascavel!" Her voice was an urgent whisper. "Open the suitcase and set up the equipment."

Cascavel, otherwise known as "Sérgio", gazed for the first time at the room they were in. The walls were covered with large, framed photos of what appeared to be a town somewhere in Latin America. There was one of a downtown area, another featuring a circular park in front of a beautiful church, and yet another of what looked like an abandoned factory that had its own particular charm. And that was just on one wall. All four walls sported such pictures. A hammock was slung from one side of the room to another. On the sturdy wooden table where Cascavel had placed the suitcase was a simple tin plate with matching cup and silverware. In the opposite corner was a waist-high sculpture of a woman, made entirely out of copper wire. Closer examination revealed it to be a remarkable representation of Francesca herself.

"I set up this room to remind me of Curvelo–my home town in Minas Gerais, Brazil," explained Francesca, seeing Cascavel's curiosity. "All the pictures are from there. The table and tableware are what were in my home when I was growing up. The sculpture was done by a local artist and given to me when my modeling career started to take off." She sighed. "When I was growing up, I did all I could to get out of there. Now, I'd do anything to get back." She stood there for a moment and Cascavel almost thought he saw tears in the former supermodel's eyes. Then she snapped out of it. "We don't have a lot of time," she said. "Let's get the equipment set up."

Cascavel opened the suitcase, reached in, and pulled out a radio receiver provided them courtesy of their friends from the Cabritan Army. He pulled up the antennae, reached in and pulled out a cassette tape recorder, and connected it by wire to the receiver. He inserted a blank cassette tape and then produced two sets of head phones. One he put on himself, and one he gave to Francesca.

"Do you think our friend on the inside will hold up his end of the deal?" he asked as he turned the dials, adjusting the frequency in search of a signal.

"I think he is very motivated to help us. We can only hope he has the courage to carry through on his end of the bargain."

Cascavel was about to comment on this when voices came through the head phones.

"This plan of yours," it was the voice of President João Ferraz, "has me a little worried."

"No need to worry. You just go about being *presidente*, and leave the worrying to me," was Santana's icy reply.

Francesca and Cascavel looked at each other in triumph. The wire under the *presidente*'s suit jacket was fully functional.

"That's all well and good for you," It was the *presidente* talking. "But remember, I'm the one who gets blamed if the whole thing goes wrong. It would make me sleep easier if I knew exactly what it is you are after with all this," insisted Ferraz. "It hurts me that after all this time, after all we've been through, that you don't trust me enough to fill me in on what is going on."

Was that a sarcastic laugh from Santana? The transmission was not clear enough for Cascavel and Francesca to be sure.

"Also," Ferraz continued, "I'm concerned about something else. Like I mentioned before, these mercenaries you brought in from outside–the Lightning Force–they're causing a lot of resentment in the regular Cabritan army. I'm afraid that there might be problems..."

"There will be no problems." Santana's voice was cold. "You, as commander and chief of Cabrito's armed forces, will see to that."

"Of course, Dr. Santana," Ferraz replied quickly. "But there are all these loose ends, and it would help me if..."

He was interrupted by the ringing of a telephone. Cascavel quickly turned the volume down until the ringing stopped, to avoid hurting their ears. When he turned it back up he heard Santana say "Excellent. That is just the kind of news I need to hear." There was the click of the phone hanging up, and then Emídio Santana's voice again. "Well, *senhor presidente*, one of those loose ends has just been tied up. Lieutenant LaRue has just confirmed the elimination of *Senhor* Raymond Sand."

In the cabin below, Cascavel and Francesca looked at each other in shock. Tears welled up in their eyes and streamed down their faces.

It wasn't the first time Max had been in a jail cell, but this one was far different than the holding tanks he had known during his wild college days, or even the dingy room he had inhabited for a week while on a top-secret mission in Eastern Europe. He had thought the Serbian cell had been lacking in the amenities, but compared to this one, somewhere in the bowels of ancient Icxi Xahn, his Belgrade prison had been The Ritz.

The walls were of thick stone skillfully fitted together. There were no windows, only a faint light from somewhere way down the hallway. It was damp, and a putrid smell hung in the air like a cloud. The door to the cell was made of a very thick, very hard wood. Max knew that, even if he had any sort of tool–which he did not–it would take him months–perhaps years–of consistent whittling to cut through the beams the held him in. There was no bed, and no place to take care of basic necessities. Max got the impression that guests didn't stay in this suite long-term.

Max got down on all fours on the cold, stone floor and began to do one-arm pushups. As the blood pumped through his body he made himself think, forcing his mind to stay active by assessing his situation. He had almost been the victim of a human sacrifice by the remnants of a very ancient civilization.

He switched to his left arm and continued thinking.

Among the celebrants of this aborted ritual were his old friend Diego and the fat old Yamani witch doctor who had tried to kill them a few months ago.

And then there was the queen–for Max was certain that was her social status. The white-skinned, green-eyed, red-haired queen of this dark-skinned, brown-eyed, black-haired tribe. How did *that* happen?

He switched to sit-ups, and his mind began to work through possible explanations for her presence on this island. Suddenly, light flooded the cell. Squinting, he leapt to his feet, ready for any chance to escape. And there, silhouetted in the opening, stood the red-haired jungle queen herself. Off to one side Max could see her burly native guard.

She fixed her emerald green eyes on him and stared for a very long time.

It worked before, he thought. *Might as well try again.*

"Amanda?" He pointed at the gold locket hanging from her neck.

She took it in her hand and rubbed her fingers over its smooth, golden surface. Max reached out his hand through the bars and motioned for her to give it to him. She recoiled, then looked at him for several moments. Max held his breath. Finally she removed the locket slowly from her neck and placed it in his hand. He kept his hands outside the wooden grate, giving her to know she could take the locket back whenever she wished. He then ran his hand over the engraved script.

"Amanda," he repeated. Then he repeated the action, and her name. She looked at him quizzically. He pointed at her and called on his limited knowledge of the Yamani tongue. "Your name... Amanda."

The jungle queen straightened and pointed at herself. "My name is Tanawehe! I am the queen of the Yamani of Icxi Xahn, daughter of Tan, the god of thunder!"

Max only understood pieces of that, but she seemed put out, and he did not want to risk losing her, not at this critical juncture. He turned the locket over in his hand, feeling the edges with his fingers. Hoping against hope, he felt until he found what he was looking for. He pressed the clasp, and the locket popped open. The queen gave a little gasp.

The color was a little faded, but the heart-shaped picture of Mr. and Mrs. Swansen was still quite visible. Mrs. Swansen's resemblance of the jungle queen in front of him was unmistakeable, and the toddler between them shared her bright red curls. Coming closer, Tanawehe examined the picture. Here eyes grew wide.

"Tanawehe!" she exclaimed, pointing to smiling, red-haired, green-eyed woman in the photo.

"No," Max shook his head, then pointed at the woman in the picture. "Mother" he said, in Yamani. Then he pointed to the fresh-faced man beside her. "Father." Then he indicated the little girl with the mop of red hair.

"Tanawehe...Amanda."

The woman grabbed the pendant from Max's hand so quickly he thought she was angry with him. But then she opened the locket again and looked at the picture. For several minutes she stood there, gazing at it in wonder. Again Max held his breath, wondering what her reaction would be. Finally she straightened up, snapped the locket closed, and barked an order. Immediately the guard stepped forward and, producing a large iron key, unlocked the ponderous gate. It creaked on its hinges as it swung open.

The queen grabbed Max by the wrist and gave some more sharp orders to the guard. Then, with determined strides, she let them through the labyrinth of stone tunnels. Their footsteps echoed through the empty chambers. After climbing what appeared to be an endless stairway they burst into the throne room, and Max found himself staring into the barrel of Diego's gun.

CHAPTER 18

DINNER AND A MOVIE

Back on the *Lua Negra* Francesca and Cascavel reeled from the shock of the horrible news they had just overheard. Ray...*dead!* Cascavel was especially hard-hit. In the days and weeks since their first less-than-friendly encounter the two had created a special bond–indeed to the younger man Ray was the father he never had. And now, he was fatherless once again. Though he tried desperately to put on a brave face, the tears refused to be held back and the sobs rose, unbidden to his throat.

"Come, Cascavel," said Francesca softly, wiping the tears from her own cheek. "We must keep our heads about us. It's what *Raimundo* would want."

She was right, and so with trembling hands and aching hearts the former Cabritan *bandido* and the former Brazilian supermodel pressed the headphones to their ears.

"My dear *presidente*," Santana was saying in the office above them. "If only you knew the scope of what is taking place."

"I know it involves not just Cabrito but Esmeralda Island as well," offered Ferraz, eager to show that he was not as far out of the loop as Santana assumed.

Santana clucked in what seemed to the eavesdroppers below like pity. "Esemeralda Island." Here he chuckled. "Esmeralda Island is of no consequence. It's what's hidden *on* Esmeralda Island that's important. After we have that, the whole place could sink into the sea, for all I care."

"And what could there be on Esmeralda Island that is so important?" asked Ferraz, as innocently as he could manage.

"That, my inquisitive friend, is on a purely need-to-know basis." There was a silence, and the clandestine listeners assumed that Ferraz must have assumed a put-out expression, because soon Santana continued: "Let me put it this way–when we have found what we are looking for on Esmeralda, you will no longer be the figurehead president of a little-known banana republic."

Francesca and Cascavel looked at each other. What did that phrase mean? Was he saying that Ferraz would no longer be president, or was he implying that whatever they found would lift the little island of Cabrito out of its international obscurity? Francesca was only too aware of the fact that keeping Cabrito relatively obscure was the long-standing official policy of the Santana clan–it allowed them to keep their shady dealings hidden from prying eyes. Generations earlier, the Santanas had been able to continue their lucrative slave trade long after it had been abandoned by most civilized nations exactly because Cabrito was generally unknown.

But now, Emídio Santana was talking about Cabrito rising from its status of virtual non-existence. Why? What would make the last in the Santana line desire such a departure from time-honored tradition?

Perhaps it was the wine he had been sipping since early in the afternoon, perhaps his desire to show just how clever he was. Whatever the case, Emídio Santana was feeling expansive that evening, and he continued his explanation with no prodding from Ferraz. "You see, my ancestors developed an ingenious and lucrative system of investing in both sides of international conflicts.

They were guaranteed payment by the winner, and in most cases were able to retrieve the original investment from the loser–and even small returns on occasion."

"International conflicts...as in, wars?"

"Indeed. They started out small...with the war for Brazilian independence against Portugal in 1822. My great-great-great grandfather Máximo Santana propped up both Dom Pedro I in Brazil and his father, Dom João, in Portugal. Later, he brought Pedro's brother Miguel back from exile and installed him as king of Portugal, and then financed Dom Pedro's expedition to Portugal to depose him. Both of these ventures proved very lucrative, so Máximo and his offspring looked for other opportunities, and found that there was no shortage of them."

"So...you mean the Santana family has been involved in..."

"Almost every major conflict since then. The Mexican-Ameircan War was the next one, then the Crimean War, followed by the American Civil War, the Prussian Wars, the Boer War, the Spanish-American War...the list goes on.

"At the end of World War One, my grandfather worked hard behind the scenes to make sure Germany would be given such unreasonable terms as to guarantee a future war on that scale or greater, and then reaped the rewards of that when World War Two broke out."

"Brilliant! Absolutely breathtaking!" exclaimed Ferraz, admiringly. "But I'm still curious: what does that have to do with Esmeralda?"

There was a pause, and the listeners below decks were afraid that Ferraz had pushed too hard in his line of questioning, and that Santana would call the meeting off prematurely. They breathed a sigh of relief as Santana continued. "During the second World War, my grandfather invested heavily in the Third Reich..."

"But Cabrito was officially on the side of the Allies!" interjected Ferraz.

"Officially...but like I said, the game has always been to play both ends against the middle. When it became evident that the Third Reich was done for, Father convinced the *Führer* that, if he would return the original investment, certain other items could be removed to Cabrito as well, with the idea that one day a new Reich would rise, phoenix-like, from the ashes of the old."

"So..." Ferraz was trying to wrap his mind around what he was hearing. You're going to revive Nazi Germany?"

"Of course not! What a stupid idea." Santana's tone was patronizing. "What's important is what Hitler left us. You've heard of his obsession with secret weapons? Well...let's just say that he was further along on his research than the rest of the world ever suspected."

"And this...this weapon or whatever it is...it's here on Cabrito?"

"On Esmeralda, actually. When they brought the original monetary investment and the...other items...back here, there was a slight mishap. The gold bullion made it ok...but the submarine carrying the secret weapons broke down near Esmeralda. The crew managed to remove everything and scuttle the sub, but then were never seen or heard from again. My grandfather convinced the Cabritan military to send an expedition after them, and they also disappeared. Finally he sent an elite squad of the Lightning Force, and they too disappeared.

"My grandfather died shortly after that, and my father, when he took over the reigns, was more interested in manipulating world markets to 'going on wild goose chases after secret Nazi weapons', as he put it."

"So why the sudden interest in whatever it is that's on Esmeralda?" the *presidente* wanted to know.

"Because a few years ago my father was going through some of the old archives, and found this."

The listeners belowdecks were clueless as to what "this" was, until Ferraz helped them out.

"A old reel of eight millimeter film?"

"And on it, one of the components my father needed in order to complete his master plan. Watch."

For a few minutes the only sound was that of the reel being placed onto an ancient projector. Santana cursed once as he tried to thread the film through the complex system of wheels and sockets. Finally the listeners heard the unmistakable *whirring* sound of the projector.

Tinny martial music played, and an announcer's voice intoned something in German that was obviously intended to impress the listener.

"What is this?" asked Ferraz.

"Official footage from the army of the Third Reich," came the answer. The German voice continued its introductory remarks. Belowdecks, Cascavel looked at Francesca, and she shook her head. German was not one of the languages she had mastered. Fortunately, back in the office, Santana came unwittingly to their rescue.

"What you are about to see," he told his guest, "is known to very few people in the world. You see, among Hitler's 'secret weapons' that he pinned his hopes on towards the end of the war were some very good ideas...ideas that, given time, could have actually worked. One of them you are about to see now. I give you the Victory Knight, or *Sieg-Ritter*, as it was known in German."

On the screen appeared a fresh-faced German soldier, surrounded by officers. Shortly the diminutive, square-moustached dictator himself came on camera and everybody gave the Nazi salute. But what caught Ferraz' attention was the man accompanying Hitler–George Santana? The pockmarked face, the stoop, the dead eyes...it took Ferraz a minute to realize that he was looking at Joaquim Santana, father to George and grandfather to Emídio. .

As the reel progressed the young German pilot was equipped with a strange looking harness. Then the camera panned to the right, and Ferraz saw *it*. At first he thought it was a medieval suit of armor, but no...it was taller by half than the young storm trooper standing next to it, and it had a modern look to it–at least what would have been considered modern in the 1940s.

"Your secret weapon is...a giant robot?" Ferraz asked, incredulously.

"Not a robot. More like a walking tank. Hitler, always one for theatrical names, called it the Victory Knight. But in this case, he wasn't exaggerating. Look."

The camera panned to the back of the metal monstrosity where two panels opened up, revealing a space large enough for a man to fit. The young German recruit gave a jaunty, stiff-arm salute, then climbed inside. A couple technicians helped snap the leather harness into place, then closed the door.

There was a slight pause, then the unearthly metal giant lurched forward. At first it's steps were jerky and ungainly, but gradually it gained a fluidity and ease of movement. On the screen, one of the generals spoke into a radio, apparently giving instructions to the man inside.

"What you are looking at is German engineering at its finest." Santana explained. There is nothing in the armor that uses any outside source of power. Everything operates according to the laws of physics, using the principles of leverage and gravity to amplify the natural movements of the man inside."

"What do you mean by 'amplify'?" Ferraz wanted to know.

"See for yourself," Santana smiled, indicating the screen.

For a few moments the metal giant executed some elementary maneuvers: running, turning, jumping–Ferraz was impressed with the agility of such a large, obviously heavy mechanism. Then the camera panned once again, revealing four storm troopers in heavy battle gear. Two of them bore field rifles, and two stood at the ready by an air-cooled machine gun. At a signal from an officer the two soldiers with rifles aimed their weapons at the mechanical giant, and the other two bent over the machine gun.

Another command came through the radio and the giant began to walk towards the guns, yet another and the soldiers commenced firing. And while it was obvious that live ammunition was being aimed directly at it, the giant took no visible damage. Rather, it continued its leisurely stroll in their direction. At a distance of about ten yards from the guns, in what could only have been a classic case of showboating, the walking suit of armor stopped, put its hands in the air, and executed a ballet-like twirl, to the delight of the onlookers. The bullets continued to bounce off its metal sides, completely ineffective.

"As you can see, this is no ordinary armor," Santana narrated. "Hitler's scientists did extensive research into hyper-resistant, yet light, alloys, and you are seeing the results. Unfortunately for him, the *Führer* lacked the extensive mining and industrial resources to mass-produce these units."

Back on the screen the armored unit had reached the machine gun. Effortlessly, it bent over, grabbed the barrel in one iron hand, and yanked upward. The two operators fell comically on their backsides as their metallic foe flipped the machine gun over its shoulder as if it were a twig.

The metal monster then turned his attention to the two riflemen. It grabbed the Mausers out of their hands and broke them at the stocks like so much kindling as the hapless soldiers looked on.

Once again the camera panned and Ferraz saw a small tank at the other end of the field, approaching the giant. It's muzzle belched fire, once, twice, three times. The camera panned back to the giant, which was walking, unharmed, towards the tank. It took a step back...obviously hit by another round, then continued forward, gathering speed as it went until it was running towards the *Panzer* unit. Ferraz was amazed at how quickly and gracefully the machine covered the distance between itself and the tank. Then, while still a few feet away, the giant executed a jump and a flip–*a flip!*–landing on its feet on top of the armored vehicle. With seemingly no effort it ripped off the metal hatch, tossed it away like a Frisbee, then reached in and pulled out a chagrined driver, depositing him unceremoniously on the ground.

With growing unease Ferraz watched the rest of the reel. The metal giant tested a variety of weapons: pulverizing, incapacitating, and otherwise neutralizing any and all targets put in front of it.

Then came the grand finale: as the small crowd of dignitaries cheered, the metal suit donned a jet pack and lifted off into the air. What followed was an animated sequence showing thousands of identical metal giants filling the skies of Europe, Asia, and the Americas.

The screen went fuzzy, Santana pressed the button on his desk, and the panels returned to their place. There was a long pause.

"*Meu Deus!*"

"So you see, my dear *presidente*, what exactly we are playing with here."

"And on Esmeralda Island is..."

"The prototype you just saw on the screen. And I don't need to tell you the kind of international power that would be wielded by the commander of an army of *those*–retrofitted with the latest technology, of course."

In the room below, Francesca and Cascavel looked at each other, shocked. Between Ferraz' questions and Santana's explanations they had a pretty good idea of what had appeared on the screen in the room above them. Though they hadn't seen the "walking tank" Santana had described, there was no doubt that it was formidable.

This was huge, though Francesca in particular was finding it difficult to grasp the enormity of what she was hearing. All this time she had thought she was married to a common robber baron, similar to the *coroneis* who had made life in her native Brazil hell for the general population a century earlier. But now she realized that she was married to a real-life super-villain, himself descended from a long line of super-villains.

"And there's more." Santana's voice crackled through the speakers again, and again the two eavesdroppers leaned in to hear what was next.

Suddenly their concentration was broken by a loud banging at the door.

"I am not to be disturbed!" Francesca put on her most commandeering tone, while at the same time she and Cascavel frantically disassembled the sound equipment. The knocking continued for a few moments, then stopped. Just as she was closing the suitcase over the incriminating machine, the door burst open, and there stood Conchita. She looked from Francesca to Cascavel and back again. Cascavel put on his most innocent expression. Francesca acted indignant.

"What is the meaning of this? Does my husband's *piranha* suddenly have the right to break into his wife's own private quarters?"

If Conchita knew that Brazilians us the term *piranha* to refer to a woman of less than virtuous character, she gave no evidence of it. Her eyes darted around the room, taking everything in. Finally they rested on the suitcase on the bed. "Open it," she ordered, curtly. It was the first time Cascavel had heard her speak, and he tried, unsuccessfully, to place the accent.

"I most certainly will not!" Francesca huffed.

Conchita produced an ugly-looking Beretta equipped with a sound suppressor. "Open it."

Francesca shrugged and bent down to open the suitcase. Slowly she pulled the zipper around and flipped open the top, revealing the sound equipment.

"Now we will go see *Senhor* Santana," Conchita said, matter-of-factly, motioning for Cascavel to pick up the suitcase.

Francesca's next movements were lightning fast. She jabbed the eject button with such force that the cassette tape inside fairly leapt out of its slot. Grabbing it in mid-air, she tossed it to Cascavel in one fluid movement. Cascavel caught it instinctively.

"Go!" Francesca ordered, and Cascavel was already on his way out the door. He heard a muffled gunshot behind him and was relieved to hear the bullet whiz past him. That meant that it hadn't found Dona Francesca.

Now he poured on all the speed he could, winding his way through the narrow corridors of the yacht. As he turned this way and that he could hear Conchita's steps behind him, and he was desperate not to present her with a clear target. Certainly she would not miss a second time.

He was beginning to lose all notion of where he was when he saw a staircase in front of him. Gambling that it would lead him to the top deck, he flew up it, and to his relief found himself out in the open, between the rail and the main cabin. Behind him he heard Conchita climbing the stairs. If he went straight, he would present his fleeing back to Conchita's pistol. To his right was the sea. To his left, a door.

He glanced over the railing at the sea, then chose the door. Opening it, he entered, slammed it shut, and turned to lock it. This completed, he turned, and his jaw fell open. There looking at him with odd expressions on their faces, were *presidente* Ferraz and Emídio Santana. Cascavel gulped.

"*Senhor Presidente, Doutor* Santana...the lady Francesca sent me up to find some...ah...caviar. And...well...I see that there is no caviar here, so I will be on my way now." He turned to open the door, but just then Conchita began rattling the door nob. "On second thought," said Cascavel to his still-stunned audience, "I think I'll leave through *that* door. Good evening!"

And not waiting another instant he dashed across the opulent office–stopping only to snag a chocolate from the jar on Santana's desk–and exited through the door on the other side, just as Conchita burst through the office door. "He has a tape!" she gasped, and immediately Santana was on his feet, the *presidente* following a short distance behind. The three of them broke out onto the deck in time to see Cascavel throw himself over the railing. There was a splash, then silence.

"Well, that's the end of him." Ferraz said.

Just then the sound of an outboard motor reached their ears. Everybody ran to the rail, and in the murky darkness below they could just make out the inflatable boat speeding away into the night. In it were Itamar and Inácio–dressed in black–and Cascavel doing his best to dry off the cassette tape by blowing on it. A few shots rang out, but the bullets smacked harmlessly into the ocean.

On the deck, Santana swore heartily. "Betrayed, by my own wife!" he exclaimed. Secretly, Ferraz considered that this betrayal was insignificant compared to Santana's own marital unfaithfulness–which had achieved legendary proportions over the years.

Santana wheeled around to face Conchita. "Get her! Bring her here now! She will pay for..."

His angry tirade was interrupted by the sound of rotors as Francesca's helicopter lifted off into the night sky. A string of ugly names erupted from Santana's mouth.

Immediately, Ferraz was on the radio he carried which gave him 24-hour access to the military command. "I want every boat in the water and every chopper in the air! You are looking for a raft on its way from the *Lua Negra*, headed towards Cabrito. The occupants are presumably armed and dangerous. They must be apprehended alive! I repeat, take them *alive!*" He looked up at Santana. "What are your wishes concerning Dona Francesca?"

Santana looked at the at the flickering light of the retreating helicopter as it winged its way towards Santo Expedito. "Don't bother. She's gone, and is of no consequence. We need to get that tape!"

"*Senhor* Santana, I'm so sorry!" Having flexed his presidential muscle by calling out the military, Ferraz was now in full grovel mode. "She called me to talk about this charity and that, and in the course of the conversation she asked if I was coming to the yacht any time soon. I mentioned that I would be coming this evening to talk some things over...I had no idea...how was I to know that the lovely *Senhora* Francesca would do something like this?"

Santana regarded his puppet president. Briefly he entertained the thought that there may have been some sort of collusion between he and Francesca, but he dismissed it as absurd. Ferraz was a coward, and a stupid one to boot. No, obviously the whole thing had been planned by the shrew of a woman he had had the misfortune of marrying. Still...it wouldn't hurt to keep Ferraz a little afraid.

"Rest assured," Santana declared, resuming his customary icy demeanor, "We will get to the bottom of this, and there will be consequences for all involved."

Ferraz gulped. "Yes, Dr. Santana," he replied. "All the resources of the Cabritan government are at your disposal."

"Of course they are," replied Santana, as if that was a foregone conclusion.

A few minutes later Francesca's chopper touched down on the roof of the Brazilian consulate in Santo Expedito. A dark-suited diplomat was there to greet her.

"*Dona* Francesca, the consul received your notice, and is delighted to receive you at the consulate. As this is officially Brazilian territory, you are safe here. Welcome home! Once you have rested, I'm sure the ambassador will want to see you."

"Thank you," she said. "My two bodyguards are Brazilian citizens, and are most likely in harms way."

"You mentioned them in your original call to us, and we have notified the Cabritan government that if they are apprehended, they are to be handed over to us immediately. Unfortunately, with regards to the Cabritan citizen you mentioned, one..." and he looked at his notes, "Cascavel, is it? As he is not Brazilian, we have no control over his situation."

"Once again, thank you for your help."

"Don't mention it, it's our job," he replied, then stood there, smiling.

"Is there anything else?" Francesca asked.

"Well..." he coughed. "My daughter has always been a big fan, and I was wondering...if you would be so kind..." He held out a piece of paper and a pen.

The rubber raft was at a standstill, moving only with the choppy waves. Above it a Cabritan Army helicopter shone a bright spotlight on its occupants. A voice cut through the noise of the propellers.

"Put your hands in the air. You are under arrest, by order of his excellency, *presidente* Osvaldo Ferraz."

In the raft, Itamar, Inácio, and Cascavel raised their hands and watched as a rope ladder descended from the aircraft.

CHAPTER 19

Max slowly raised his hands. Diego had the pistol pointed straight at his chest, and he looked to be in a very foul mood. To their left Queen Tanawehe was exchanging sharp words with the fat witch doctor, who, Max noticed, was sitting on the throne.

"I bet you're wondering what they're talking about," Diego said with an evil grin. "Well, for your information, the queen is a little upset that my friend the witch doctor is sitting on her throne. She is finding out right now that, in her absence, Owanalehe was able to convince her royal guard the she is a demon that has been tricking them for years, and that, to make amends, she is to be sacrificed, along with you, at the earliest possible moment."

How does that fat slob have such a hold over the Yamani? Max wondered to himself.

Diego seemed to read his mind. "It's the Green Monkey," he said, indicating with his head a necklace that hung around what passed for Owanalehe's neck. Sure enough, from the chain hung an emerald carved in the form of an sinister-looking monkey. "It's what you call a totem. The Yamani believe it contains powerful spirits, and the one who wields it has tremendous authority. My Yamani grandmother used to tell me fantastic stories about the terrible fate that overtook those who dared to disobey the will of the bearer of the Green Monkey. Fortunately for us, the Shadow People have not forgotten this particular bit of nonsense."

It was all Max could do not to roll his eyes. This Diego character was all swagger. If he didn't have a gun in his hand he would be running like the coward he was.

After a brief yet sharp exchange between the witch doctor, the queen, and the two warriors who had accompanied them, the warriors grabbed Tanawehe's arms and pinned them behind her back.

So much for loyalty to the crown Max mused. *If only there was some kind of distraction...*

As if on cue, Tanawehe let out a blood-curdling scream. Everyone in the room turned their attention to her. Everyone, that is, except Max. Taking advantage of the brief turn of Diego's head, he pounced, grabbed the soldier's wrist with one hand, applying increasing pressure, and relieved him of his gun with the other, all in one swift motion."

"Get him! Get Missionary Ma..."

Diego's desperate howl was brought short by the retort of the pistol as Max shot him in the foot. Diego let out a scream that matched Tanawehe's in volume and pitch, and exceeded it in sheer pain. Max stepped to the queen's side and pointed at the others–one at a time–with the pistol. Nobody moved. At least for the moment, the loaded weapon carried more power than the Green Monkey.

But it was only for a moment. Suddenly the doors to the throne room opened and *onça* skin-clad guards poured in and surrounded Max and Tanawheh, spears leveled. Max realized that he could shoot one or two of them, but there was no way he could take on the entire crowd. Slowly he placed the pistol on the stone floor and raised his hands in surrender. Tanawhehe followed suit, although her lips remained curled in disdain.

"Get them out of here!" Diego screamed, hopping up and down on one foot.

Minutes later, Max found himself back in the dank cell where he had spent the night. In the next cell over he could hear the snarling imprecations of the red-headed jungle queen.

Silence had fallen over the jungle camp, and Mary Sue had drifted off to sleep by the warm fire. Suddenly her eyes flew open. There was a hand on her shoulder! Her scream was stifled by another hand over her mouth. Then there was a whisper in here ear.

"It's ok...it's me, Ilana. I managed to get free, and now we're going to get out of here."

Mary Sue nodded, and Ilana released her hand from the girls mouth. "We don't have much time," she continued. "The sentry is on the other side of the camp, but he'll be back before long." She extended her hand to Mary Sue. The American girl did not take it.

"You!" she said, accusingly. Ilana looked around her frantically to see if the girl's voice had been heard. The camp remained still.

"Shhhhh!" she whispered. "Come on...we can talk later!"

"You have bewitched my Maxwell. You have turned him against me...made him want to stay in this God-forsaken place full of heathens and...and criminals."

"Please!" Ilana was near tears. "Keep your voice down..."

"I will NOT keep my voice down! I'm on to you...you jungle tramp! You want to get me killed, possibly even get Max killed. Well I'm not going to let it happen." Then, to Ilana's utter dismay she rose to her feet and let out a yell. "GUARDS! The prisoner is trying to escape!"

Light's flashed on all throughout the camp. Stunned, Ilana stared at the American girl, who was looking back at her in smug triumph.

"Why...?"

Immediately the two women were surrounded by soldiers. Mary Sue pointed her finger at Ilana imperiously. "She was trying to escape and take me with her!" she accused. Still in shock, Ilana was dragged back through the camp and re-fastened to the tree, this time with twice as much rope, and so tightly she had difficulty breathing.

"You have rendered us a great service, Mary Sue." It was Captain Sanchez. He flashed her a brilliant smile. "I will make certain that you are compensated for your efforts."

The camp settled down again, and Mary Sue drifted back to sleep, content in the belief that she had saved the day. Meanwhile, on the other side of the camp, Ilana seethed, tears of anger streaming unimpeded down her face, even as the ropes bit into her with every breath she took.

The helicopter touched down, the rotors slowed to a stop, and the hydraulic doors opened with a *hiss*. Even though he was blindfolded, Cascavel knew exactly where he was. The stench that emanated from the Cabrito Federal Corrections Facility made Cascavel want to throw up. Before his conversion he had spent more time there than he cared to remember, and the very idea of being there again filled his heart with dread.

Guards grabbed him roughly from behind and pushed out of the helicopter. Still bound, he fell in a heap on the ground. Then the guards grabbed him by both arms and lifted him to his feet. Struggling to regain his footing, they pushed him forward. Still blindfolded, he could sense the change in atmosphere when he went through the door of the prison. With growing despair he heard the door shut behind him with an ominous "clang", and then he was moving again, compelled by the unseen hands that gripped his arms.

He heard another door open, and then, without warning, he was thrown onto a hard cement floor...then, curiously, lifted into a chair. His blindfold was whipped off and he blinked. He was sitting in a square room, furnished with one table and two chairs. A single light-bulb hung from the ceiling, barely illuminating Cascavel and the two guards at either side of him.

The door opened and two men and a woman walked in. Cascavel recognized them immediately: Emídio Santana, Presidente Ferraz, and Conchita. The uniforms on either side of him saluted, then took up positions beside the door. Santana took the chair opposite Cascavel, while Ferraz remained standing. In Santana's hand was a folder, which he opened on the table in front of him.

"So, I have the pleasure of addressing *senhor* Cascavel, or..." and here he glanced at the file in front of him, "Nixon." He looked up at the miserable man in front of him. "Seriously? Your mother named you Nixon? I suppose now you're going to tell me that you are not a crook."

Cascavel looked at his tormentor blankly, the allusion lost on him. Ferraz gave a forced chuckle. "Good one, sir."

Santana sighed and shook his head. "Let's get this over with. Hand over the cassette tape, please."

"What cassette tape?" Cascavel asked, innocently.

"Don't play games with us," snarled Santana. "Conchita here saw Francesca flip the cassette to you. We searched the raft, and the two Brazilians, and it was nowhere to be found. That means that it has to be with you. So, hand it over."

"I know nothing of any cassette," Cascavel insisted, stubbornly. Santana rolled his eyes and motioned to one of the soldiers, who stepped forward and, in one swift motion, ripped off Cascavel's shirt. The cassette tape that had been hidden within fell to the floor. The guard picked it up and handed it to Santana.

"Oh, you mean *that* cassette tape." Cascavel grinned, sheepishly. Santana motioned to one of the soldiers, who stepped forward and smacked Cascavel across the face. Then Santana snapped his fingers and the other soldier set a tape player on the table in front of him.

Santana held up the tape, making a show of examining it by every angle. "It's truly ironic, *senhor* Nixon, that you too will be brought down by a secret recording."

Again, there was an uncomfortable pause as it became painfully evident that Cascavel–aka Nixon–knew absolutely nothing about his infamous namesake. Finally Santana flipped open the lid of the cassette player and, a little dramatically, inserted the tape, rewound it to the beginning, and pushed "play".

There was a slight pause, then from the device emanated the sound of a driving rhythm accompanied by electric guitar. Santana looked up at Cascavel in surprise. Presently, the voices of five adolescent boys filled the room.

"*Ven claridad, llega ya, amanece de una vez claridad, por piedad mata sombras, dame luz, resplandor, libertad...*"

"What is this?" Santana fairly screamed.

"If I'm not mistaken sir, it's Menudo," responded Ferraz, barely able to restrain his smile.

"*Para no soñarla más, no ya no, nunca mas que vuelvo a su esclavitud...*" continued the voices.

"I *know* who it is!" Santana raged. "Who doesn't know who Menudo is? What I don't know is *why* I am here in the Cabrito Federal Corrections Facility listening to a Puerto Rican boy band from the '80s." He turned and pointed his finger at Cascavel. "YOU! You sneak onto my yacht, run away holding this tape, and when we catch you and play the tape, its...its...*Menudo!*"

"*Ven claridad, quédate, y no vuelvas a escapar no te lleves el sol...*"

Out of the corner of his eye, Cascavel thought he caught one of the soldiers moving, ever so slightly, to the latino-rock rhythm.

"*Maldito...!*" Santana jabbed his finger at the keys, trying to stop the music. Instead he hit the fast-forward button, which sped up the tape, making it sound like "Menudo Meets the Chipmunks". Growing more and more frustrated, he poked at the keys a few more times, to no effect. At last he grabbed the machine and flung it across the room.

"*Que no quiero recordar su figura su voz cada noche que...*" The music stopped abruptly as the cassette player shattered against the wall.

Santana glared at Cascavel. "Well?"

Cascavel put his wrists together and held them up to Santana as in a gesture of submission, a doleful look on his face.

"It's true, I'm guilty." He said, mournfully. "I'm guilty of having terrible musical taste. I've liked Menudo since I was a boy. Many times I tried to break the addiction, but it just came back, stronger than ever."

Santana's mouth hung open in shock. Behind him, Ferraz had to pinch himself—hard—in order to keep from laughing out loud.

"But in my defense," Cascavel continued, then pointed dramatically at the guard closest to him, "I saw that guy swaying to the music just now!"

Ferraz would have burst out laughing at that one, had Santana not brought his hand down so hard on the table that everybody jumped.

"Enough!" He stood up and bent over the table, bringing himself face-to-face with Cascavel. "I don't know what you think you are pulling off here, but believe me, you will wish with all your might that you had never gotten mixed up in this business. You are a vagabond, a peon, a *nothing*, and I will squash you like the insignificant insect that you are, just like I will squash everybody else who tries to get in my way."

He straightened up. "Guards, take him away. Put him somewhere where he will never see the light of day."

As he was being led out of the room and through the dank halls of the prison, Cascavel's heart was as light as a feather. He actually found himself whistling the catchy melody of *Claridad*, and was quite sure the guard behind him was humming along.

CHAPTER 20

TRUE COLORS

Day broke over the jungle camp, and when Mary Sue awoke, her "forest ranger" friends were already in motion, striking the tents and packing their equipment. As she stood up and stretched, she saw Ilana being herded to one end of the camp. The island girl shot her a reproachful look as she passed, and Mary Sue felt the slightest twinge of guilt.

Then, without warning she was grabbed from behind by rough hands. Before she knew what was happening she was bound, just as she had been the previous day, and was being shoved toward Ilana.

"Hey!" she yelled, when she found her voice. "Lieutenant Sanchez said I was to be treated with the greatest courtesy. What is the meaning of this?"

"It means," the voice of the Argentine purred smoothly nearby, "that you have outlived your usefulness to us."

"What? I thought..."

"Yesterday we believed you could help us find Mr. Sherman. This morning we received word that he has already been captured. Hence, we no longer need your services in helping bring him to us." He smiled the same warm smile he had flashed her last night. "When the fish is caught, there is no need for the bait."

"What...what are you going to do with me now?"

Sanchez shrugged. "If I had my way I would dispatch you."

"Dispatch...you mean..."

"Yes, just like we did with those savages traveling with you yesterday. Unfortunately for me, we have orders to bring you and the other girl with us, so you get a slight reprieve. Unless I miss my guess, however, those three unfortunate Indians probably got the better end of the deal."

"Where...where are we going?" she stammered.

"We're on our way to Icxi Xahn. You and your friend will be turned over to the folks there. I understand they have creative ways of getting rid of unwanted guests." Again he smiled, and for the first time the American girl noticed the cruelty behind his eyes.

It was all too much for Mary Sue, and she passed out.

The morning sun glinted off the snow in the farm-country of Upstate New York. Regina Sherman sat in the simple kitchen and wolfed down some of the best pancakes she had ever eaten.

"The syrup comes from maple trees out back. We tap them ourselves, and boil the syrup down. This is last-year's batch, we'll start again in February."

A mere forty-eight hours earlier Regina would have been bored silly by talk of maple trees, sugar season, or pancakes. But much had changed yesterday. Her business empire had come crashing down around her, she had found herself with nowhere to turn, and–adding insult to injury–she had managed to get herself stranded in a snow drift in the middle of Upstate cow country.

Now she was grateful for the fact that Pastor Dave had found her, that he and his wife had given her a warm place to sleep, and this delicious breakfast. She even found the folksy chatter from Linda, Pastor Dave's wife, to be strangely comforting.

In the excitement of the previous night she had explained very little about herself or what she was doing in Greensborough. While they were towing her car to the garage she had mentioned that she was from the city and on her way to visit family. Thankfully they hadn't pried any further.

After taking care of the car, Dave had gone to help the farmer round up his wayward cows. Linda had served Regina some soup–homemade chicken noodle–and showed her to the spare bedroom. Regina didn't realize how exhausted she really was until she lay out on the bed. Within seconds she was fast asleep.

The smell of breakfast had woken her up. Putting on the bathrobe Linda had provided, she had padded into the kitchen to find her place set and a steaming pile of pancakes awaiting her.

"Takes several hours to boil the sap down into syrup. When it's done, though, it sure tastes a lot better than that store-bought stuff."

Regina nodded, her mouth full of the delicious pancakes.

"If you look there on the fridge, you'll see some pictures we took last spring when we were boiling the sap."

Regina glanced up at the refrigerator, and froze. Indeed there were several pictures from last-year's maple syrup season, but she didn't even notice them. Here eyes were focused on the picture off to the side and a little below, held in place by a magnet shaped like the letter "M".

The picture was of her son.

"Regina, are you okay?" Linda had stopped when she saw her guest staring, open mouthed at the refrigerator.

Regina closed her mouth, swallowed the remaining pancake, then spoke quietly. "Why do you have a picture of my son?"

Now it was Linda's turn to be surprised. "Max is your son? Honey, come here!" This last to her husband, who was just returning from shoveling the driveway.

"What is it, Linda?"

"How...do you know my son?" Regina asked, slowly. "Maxwell Sherman...my son," she repeated.

The next several minutes were a jumble of excited talk and comparing notes. Pastor Dave and his wife filled Regina in on a portion of her son's life that she had missed almost entirely. Regina, in turn, shared with them about Max's background, something he had always seemed reluctant to discuss with them.

After about an hour, their conversation turned to current events.

"So you say you have no way of getting in touch with him now?"

"None whatsoever," sighed Regina. "Before I would communicate through James–my liaison in Cabrito–but now even he is incommunicado."

The more they talked, the more concerned Pastor Dave was growing. "Did you know that Max's girlfriend, Mary Sue, is down there with him?"

"Girlfriend? But I thought..."

"You thought what?"

"Oh, never mind. Mothers can read too much into things sometimes."

"Well, whatever the case, I was talking to her parents the other day. They said they haven't heard from her since Saturday. Before she was calling–collect–every day."

"Yeah and this whole thing went down on Monday...yesterday."

"So what do you think this is all about?" Linda wanted to know.

Regina sighed. "It's a long story. Years ago, my husband had some dealings with George Santana–normal business deals, or at least, so he thought. In the process, however, he stumbled upon some rather damaging information about Mr. Santana. It's kind of complicated, but it involved financial corruption of a high order. He went to meet Santana to talk about it at a little cabin we own in Saratoga Springs. It was on his way back to New York from there that he was killed in a freak car accident."

"I'm so sorry!" Linda commiserated.

Pastor Dave asked "Did they find anything at the scene?"

"No papers of any kind, if that's what you mean. When they recovered Theo's body, they found a Boy Scout knife in his hand–the one he used when he and Max went fishing and exploring. Max had an identical one."

"And did anybody ever investigate George Santana?"

"The police opened an investigation, then shut it down almost immediately, alleging that they had nothing to go on."

"But you don't believe them."

"Let's just say that I've been carrying on my own private investigation ever since, but it has turned up nothing of note. George Santana has covered his tracks very well. In the mean time, I've played nice with him, even investing heavily in our Cabrito venture. I also sent my best and most loyal man–James Rockwell–there with instructions to keep his ear to the ground.

"Then, a couple months ago, I was forced to intervene in a tense situation involving my son on the runway at the Santo Expedito International Airport. When I showed up, Max was staring down the wrong end of a pistol held by Emídio."

"Who's Emídio?" Linda wanted to know

"He's George Santana's spoiled son. He pretty much runs things on Cabrito."

"Max mentioned that incident on the runway in one of our phone conversations," said Pastor Dave. "It still blows me away that your son ended up on the same island where you were opening a factory–and the two events had nothing to do with each other.".

"Yes, it was quite a coincidence, wasn't it."

"Oh, I didn't say it was a coincidence, just that it blows me away. I don't believe in coincidence."

Regina smiled tightly. "Be that as it may, I put in a quick call to George and told him in no uncertain terms that, if he didn't call off his boy, all kinds of information he had been hiding would hit the fan. It worked, although I was mostly bluffing. I remember thinking, at that point, that the whole thing might come back to bite me. Well, yesterday, it did. And my son..." Regina broke into tears again.

Linda reached across the table and put a hand on her shoulder. Pastor Dave was thoughtful. "You say there's no way to get in touch with Max right now?"

Regina Sherman nodded.

"Ok...but...what if we started working on another angle."

"What do you mean?"

"Do you have access to the information your husband had on George Santana?"

Regina shook her head. "No. He never told me. Nothing was found in his car..."

"But Santana thinks you have it, because if he didn't you wouldn't have had any leverage on him on the runway." Pastor Dave completed her thought.

"Right," Regina affirmed. Suddenly she stood up. "Listen, I appreciate your hospitality and all, but I really should be going. There is no doubt that George Santana is tracking me somehow, and if he is I'm putting you all in danger."

Pastor Dave smiled. "You're not going anywhere. We love Max, and that love extends to his mother as well."

"But George Santana is not a man to be trifled with!" exclaimed Regina.

Pastor Dave smiled. "I'm sure that's the case, but I think you might be underestimating us country folk." He reached for the phone on the wall and dialed a number. "Hello, Millard? We have Max's mother here at our house, and it's possible that she could be in some kind of danger. Can you put the word out for people to be aware of any suspicious activity? Thanks. Let us know if you hear anything." He hung up the phone and smiled. "That will buy us a few hours at least. Now...let's talk about the chalet in Saratoga Springs."

CHAPTER 21

FRANKLY, MY DEAR

A mist rose over the ancient stone structures of Icxi Xahn. Through the mist marched Lieutenant Sanchez and his elite squad of Lightning Troopers, two bound women in their midst. They were met at the entrance to the inhabited part of the city by a troop of the *onça* skin-clad warriors of the Shadow People, who escorted them down the main avenue. As they penetrated further into the ancient city, a crowd began to gather, sensing what was about to happen. Their bloodlust had gone unslaked yesterday, and now they were pleased to see that today there would be more victims to quench their unholy thirst.

In the centuries since their re-possession of the ancient Yamani capital the Shadow People had been content with animal sacrifices to appease the capricious gods they served with fear. Yet as they slowly reclaimed the ruins from the ever-encroaching jungle they could not help but notice the grotesque carvings on temple walls and monuments–carvings that depicted brutal human sacrifices in all their gory details. And then there was the centerpiece of the city–the immense half-pyramid topped by an altar still stained with human blood, even after centuries of disuse. It's very presence seemed to mock the Shadow People. *You're not doing enough! Your puny animal sacrifices cannot possibly appease gods who have had a taste of human blood.*

There was much rejoicing, therefore, at the arrival of Tanawehe, sent directly from heaven by the fire god Tan. What more evidence did they need of divine favor?

And then the fat witch-doctor had arrived, carrying with them that feared relic from their shadowy past, and telling them of evil intentions of their long-lost Yamani brethren. But not to fear, Owanalehe himself would lead them into battle–accompanied by that fearful talisman–and victory would be assured, *if* the appropriate sacrifice were made first.

That night the drums had throbbed so loudly that the screams of the wretched prisoner bound to the altar could barely be heard. And when Owanalehe lifted the still-beating heart into the air for all to see, the crowd–fortified by papaya alcohol and frenzied by the incessant rhythm- screamed its approval.

And when the warriors returned with stories of overwhelming victory and great feats of war, the conclusion was obvious: *we need to sacrifice more humans.* Yesterday had been a letdown, but today's fresh supply of victims proved to more than make up for it.

As the two unfortunate women were herded through the city, the observant among the Shadow People noted the outstanding differences between the two. First, there was the pale one, dressed in strange clothes, and with the demeanor of someone who was completely defeated. She walked hunched over, her once glorious blond hair now matted and stringy as it fell down over her face. At one point she stumbled and fell to the ground. The crowd howled with delight.

The other young woman was obviously Yamani–although she was not of the Shadow People. Though bound, she walked erect, her face set, her eyes alert. Her *onça* skin garb matched that of the warriors who surrounded her.

With the logic of a bloodthirsty mob, the spectators came to the conclusion that the dark girl could only be a witch sent over to exact revenge for their raid, and that she had enlisted the help of the other woman–also a witch. Fortunately for the residents of Icxi Xahn, the awesome power of Owanalehe and the Green Monkey had overcome them.

Ilana had heard about the mysterious Shadow People her whole life and so, despite the dire circumstances, she could not help but be fascinated by what she was seeing. The legends were true, she realized–not just the ones about the departure of the sept of Yamani known as the River People, but also the even older legends about the city of Icxi Xahn itself.

As they continued through the city she noticed the absence of new constructions. The Shadow People had not built anything new, they had simply appropriated the older structures left by their ancestors...cannibalizing them as needed to fit their current needs. The Shadow People, she realized, were not an urban people, but a jungle people dwelling in the midst of ancient urban ruins.

A sob from her companion brought her mind back to their current predicament. She looked over at the pitiful figure next to her. The American girl had come completely undone. She had been crying uncontrollably since they'd left the camp that morning, finally settling down to low sobs and moans as they approached the city. Ilana had been busy trying to think through the situation, and so the two had not talked.

"Why?" Mary Sue moaned. "Why is this happening to me? What did I do to deserve this?"

Ilana was tempted to remind her that, if it hadn't been for Mary Sue's stupid actions of last night, they both could have escaped. But a sidelong glance at the broken girl beside her moved her heart to pity.

"Try to stay calm," she whispered. "I know how my people think, and trust me, it's better if you don't show fear."

Mary Sue looked up at Ilana, her eyes red from crying. "It's hopeless," she said. "They're going to kill us. It doesn't matter what we do now."

"It's not hopeless," whispered Ilana, trying to maintain her stoic demeanor for the crowds while at the same time comforting the distraught girl beside her. "Max is still out there somewhere."

At the mention of Max's name, Mary Sue let out another wail. "No, he's not!" she blubbered. "Commander Sanchez told me this morning that he has been captured. He's probably dead by now. My Max is dead, and it's all your fault!"

And that was the last straw for Ilana. This clueless girl had insisted on coming along on this expedition, had gone over to the enemy, had thwarted her escape, and now was blaming her for all their problems.

"Listen, you air-headed little 'daddy's girl'," she hissed. Mary Sue's jerked up at the harsh tone. Ilana continued, her anger growing. "Ever since the day we met in the airport, you have looked down on me. I'm not good enough, I'm not Christian enough, I'm not American enough. But let me tell you this, I lived in America for four years, and met many people who called themselves Christian–but none of them, *not one of them*, ever acted any different from anybody else. They were all just like you, content with their comfortable lives, looking down their noses at everybody."

Ilana couldn't tell if her words were having any effect, but she was warming to her subject. "The first real Christian I met was Max, and I supposed that his girlfriend would be someone like him. But I was wrong. You are just like all the others. Max told me once that some people who called themselves Christians had never actually met Christ. And now, having met you, I'm sure he was right. You're nothing but a phony, and if it's true that we're going to die in a few moments, you might want to get right with Jesus."

"Wh...but..." Mary Sue's stunned sputtering was cut mercifully short as the procession turned the corner. They found themselves in a large square, packed with people. A roar went up from the crowd, and they separated to form a path for the newcomers. At the end of that path loomed a pyramid with stairs leading to its apex. Somewhere behind them drummers began hammering out a slow, hypnotic rhythm. But Ilana barely heard them. Instead her eyes were fixed on the top of the pyramid, and what she saw there made her catch her breath and temporarily lose her stoic bearing.

Mary Sue looked up at that moment and let out a shriek.

"Max!"

Millard Fenton, a portly, retired farmer who divided his free time between his grandkids and numerous hobbies, was shoveling his driveway when a black Cadillac pulled up and stopped. The passenger window rolled down and a friendly-looking, blond-haired man poked his head out. "Excuse me, sir. Do you know where this address is? My GPS has been sending me around in circles." He handed Millard a scrap of paper. The older gentleman removed his cap and scratched his snowy-white head as he looked at the address. It was the address for Pastor Dave's house. He gave the occupants of the car a once-over, and didn't like what he saw. Something about these two fellows just didn't sit right with him.

"So, can you tell us how to get there?"

"Yep, sure can," was the reply. This was followed by a long, awkward pause.

"Well...what are you waiting for?" The man didn't sound quite so friendly now.

"Just because I *can* tell you where it is, doesn't mean I'm *going* to tell you where it is."

"What?"

"You heard me. Now get along before I call the cops on you for loitering. And don't think they won't come. The chief of police is my son-in-law."

Swearing, the man rolled up the window and the car pulled away, tires spinning on the slushy pavement. Millard watched them go, then walked back to his garage and opened the door that led to his basement. He descended the stair case, favoring the leg that had been sore since Korea, walked over to the far side of his electric train layout, and opened a large case propped up against the wall. From the impressive array of firearms contained therein he picked out a Colt 45 and a 12-gauge shotgun that had sealed the fate of many a woodchuck foolish enough to step onto the Fenton property. Holstering the pistol in his belt, he picked up his cell phone (a modern nuisance his overprotective kids had insisted on him having ever since he had slipped on the ice and broken a rib two winters ago) and made a couple quick calls. Then he went back up the stairs to the garage, got into his restored 1953 Ford pickup, and backed out of the driveway.

Pastor Dave hung up the phone. "That was Millard. He says we've got company."

"Is he okay?" asked Linda.

"Fine. The guys have things under control, but it's time for us to move out."

"We'll take the Bentley!" said Regina, standing up. The fire was back in her eyes, and, had there been any doubt before, there could be none now that Maxwell Sherman was her son.

Pastor Dave smiled. "Meaning no disrespect to the British car-makers, but the way we're going will tear your vehicle into pieces within minutes. We'll need to travel a little lighter." Minutes later Regina–bundled in a bulky snowsuit that made her feel rather like Buzz Aldrin–was hanging for dear life to Pastor Dave's waist as his snowmobile flew over the snow-covered pastures and cornfields. She had long since lost her bearings, but Pastor Dave navigated the machine with a confidence that bordered on recklessness. Determined not to show any more weakness to this friend of her son, Regina set her jaw and lowered her head against the wind.

CHAPTER 22

DISORGANIZED RELIGION

Maxwell Sherman had been in tight spots before. His commanding officers in the Green Berets had noticed right away his talent in combat, and had singled him out for specialized training. After this had come special assignments in "hot" zones around the world where combat skills and a knack for survival came in very handy. There had been many occasions where he and his "battle buddies" had survived by the narrowest of margins.

Even in his short time on Cabrito, the cards had been stacked against him on numerous occasions. Yet standing on top of the sacred pyramid of Icxi Xahn, he was having a difficult time remembering a time when the situation had looked quite so grim.

In such circumstances Max's mind was trained to break the problem down into steps which would lead to survival–the first step being a list of advantages and disadvantages. Such an exercise was proving difficult in this case due to a complete lack of advantages. He was at the top of the massive stone structure, arms bound tightly behind him. Next to him was the ever defiant jungle queen—Tanawehe—bound the same way. Her continuous verbal assaults on the numerous guards only seemed to amuse them.

Stationed at the four corners of the platform were four warriors, their spears at ready. Diego and the fat witch doctor were there also–Diego limping, his wounded foot bandaged up with rags. Both of them, however, seemed to be enjoying themselves immensely.

Even if Max and Tanawehe were to somehow break free of their bonds *and* overwhelm the guards, they would have two options: confront the bloodthirsty mob below or try to thread their way through the caves under hot pursuit.

Max found himself wishing he spoke the Yamani tongue so he could communicate with the wildcat next to him, perhaps she could clue him in to some sort of foothold.

Note to self, he thought grimly. *If I get out of this mess, I will learn Yamani.*

The way it seemed to him, the minus column was full, and the plus column was empty. If he could just add *one* item to that plus column...

Suddenly there was some sort of disturbance in the crowd below. Max saw the multitude part at the edge of the square, and saw the small troop enter–machine-gun toting soldiers surrounded by jungle warriors. And in the middle: Ilana and Mary Sue.

Uncontrolled emotions surged briefly in Max's chest–relief that the girls were still alive, terror of what might be in store for them, helplessness to do anything about it. Doggedly he fought them down and forced his mind to think. While he was happy she was still alive, the presence of Mary Sue would complicate things more. But with Ilana here there was now a way to communicate with Tanawehe. *Chalk one up to the plus column!*

Max watched as they ascended the stairway–Mary Sue hunched over, defeated, terrified; Ilana erect and resolute. Finally they reached the top.

"Hello ladies!" Max said, trying to force a grin and a nonchalant attitude.

"Oh Max! This is so terrible! What are they going to do to us?" Mary Sue wailed. Diego heard the outburst and hobbled over to where the prisoners were gathered.

"Welcome to our little party!" he beamed, speaking in English so Mary Sue would be sure to understand. "Our guests are all present,"–here he indicated the crowd surging at the foot of the pyramid–"and the entertainment–that's you–has arrived."

"How nice of you to invite us!" said Max. "Must be tough playing host, with your foot and all." As he motioned with his head towards Diego's wounded appendage his eyes fell briefly on the weapon holstered at Diego's waist–a Taurus PT 24&7, the sidearm favored by the Brazilian armed forces. It was a powerful piece of hardware, with a magazine capable of holding 12 bullets. But what interested Max more was that the holster that held it was unfastened.

Very careless, Diego. Max thought. *One more for the plus column.*

"Your confidence fools nobody," Diego snarled. "You will not be so brave once you have watched all your friends be sacrificed alive on that altar." His hand swept in the direction of the blood-stained table that occupied center-stage at the top of the pyramid. "By the time it gets to be your turn, you will be crying like a little baby."

"Diego," Max replied evenly, "I just have one question for you."

"What's that?"

"How's your foot?" and with that Max brought his booted heel down hard on Diego's already wounded appendage. Diego howled in pain, jumping up and down and cursing. Below, the crowd roared in laughter.

That probably didn't add anything to the plus column, but it sure was fun. Max thought.

Owanalehe stepped to the front a raised his hand to quiet the crowd. Shooting a dirty look at Max and his friends, Diego hobbled over to join the witch doctor. In a loud, pompous voice, he began addressing the crowd. Max slid closer to Ilana.

"Who's the redhead?" she asked.

"She was the queen here, until our fat friend convinced the guards she was evil."

"Let me guess...the Green Monkey?"

"Exactly. Now listen, see if you can calm her down and talk to her. She might know something that can help us get out of here."

"Got it." Ilana shifted her position until she could talk to Tanawehe, who was desperately squirming against the ropes. When she heard the words in her own tongue the queen calmed down. As Ilana talked to her under her breath, Max worked hard on his solution.

The Lightning Troopers had declined to make the climb up the pyramid, and were standing below at the edge of the crowd. They would be unable to interfere immediately in any action that took place. Max added that to the plus column, and continued thinking. His thoughts were interrupted by a chant that started to come from the crowd.

Laka Woh

Laka Woh

At first it was just a few people shouting it out, then it spread and grew until the words surged forth in unison from the rabid throng.

LAKA WOH!

LAKA WOH!

Max looked over at Ilana.

"He asked who they wanted him to sacrifice first, and that's their answer."

"Who?"

Ilana hesitated. "Golden hair."

All eyes turned to Mary Sue. Her mouth fell open, then her eyes rolled back in her head, her knees buckled, and she sank to the stone floor. Two guards stepped in, yanked her up by the arms, and dragged her over to the altar.

"Noooooooo...." she moaned. The crowd below was beside itself with frenzy.

"Did you get anywhere with the queen?" Max hissed.

"She says there's a way out, if we can get free. She didn't tell me how..."

"I hope she's right."

Mary Sue was bent over the altar, facing the crowd. The warriors had revived her from her faint, and her horrified eyes saw the mob below dancing and leaping with glee. The disgusting priest held her head up by her long blond hair. He raised his knife in the air for a brief second, then brought it down...

SLASH!

It sliced effortlessly through the poor girl's long locks, and she fell face down onto the altar. The priest held the severed hair up for all to see, and spasms of laughter overcame the crowd. Everybody's attention was on the bizarre scene in front of them. Even Diego was jumping up and down on his one good foot.

"It's now or never." Max hissed, and Ilana nodded grimly.

Before the warrior nearest them could react Max and Ilana acted at the same time. Max dropped and rolled, Ilana jumped into the air. Max's roll caught one of the guards at the heels and he fell, his spear clattering to the ground beside him. He groped for it, but Tanawehe, who was quick to grasp what was going on, stepped on it with one foot, and delivered a devastating kick to his face with the other, causing him to fall to the ground heavily.

Meanwhile Max came out of his roll and to his feet right next to Diego. He stood up, twisted around, and grabbed Diego's revolver from its holster. Taking a split second to calculate he squeezed off a shot which caught the surprised Diego in his good foot. Once again Diego screeched in pain, crumpling to the flagstones and holding his newly injured foot.

Ilana had landed lightly on her feet, inches from where the fat witch-doctor stood. She sprung nimbly into the air again and planted a bare foot with all the force she could muster into the small of Owanalehe's back. He yelled in surprise, released his grip on the hair *and* the knife, and went tumbling–or rather, rolling–down the stone stairway.

With lightning quickness Ilana rolled to the ground and grabbed the knife. Max saw this action and rolled towards her. They stood at the same time, back to back. Looking behind her, Ilana brought the knife down in one swift motion, and it severed the ropes that bound him. He wheeled, grabbed the knife, and freed Ilana.

Then they both turned back towards Tanawehe. The jungle queen was crouched on top of the fallen spear, surrounded by three warriors whose spears were pointed at her. She was jumping, yelling, and generally making a scene, and Max realized with appreciation that she was doing this to give himself and Ilana as much time as possible.

Lifting the pistol Max put a bullet into the shoulder of one of the guards closest to the red-head. The report of the shot and the scream of the victim made the other guards shrink back, temporarily causing confusion. Ilana leapt to the queen's side, Max threw the knife to her, and with one stroke Tanawehe was free. As befitting royalty, she immediately took charge.

"Come this way!" she said in Yamani, and Ilana motioned to Max. To Max's surprise she dashed straight to the altar, where Mary Sue was still draped over the surface. Lifting the other girl with amazing ease, she placed one foot on the side of the large stone and pushed. Catching her drift, Max and Ilana joined her. At first there were no results. Out of the corner of his eye Max saw Owanalehe stirring about halfway down the pyramid, where his fall had ended. Diego was still wallowing in pain and cursing. The remaining two guards were approaching cautiously, mindful of the firearm still in Max's hand.

Suddenly a bullet winged overhead. Sanchez and the Lightning Force had finally realized what was happening and were trying to take matters in their own hands. For now they were impeded by the crowd, but Max had no doubt that one of them would get a good line of fire sooner or later, and then it would be all over.

Max threw all of his weight against the stone altar, and finally it budged. A small crack appeared in the flagstone floor. Again he pushed, and it moved a little farther. Bullets zinged past, and Max made a final push. The altar slid all the way open, revealing a tunnel that descended straight down into the darkness below. Hand and foot grips had been carved into the rock countless years ago.

"Quick, get down the hole!" Max urged. Tanawehe went first, still carrying the limp Mary Sue. Ilana was next.

"Come on, Max!" she urged.

"Just a second!" He yelled back. "I'm going to get some insurance." He stuck the pistol into the waistband of his pants and, crouching low, ran over to where Diego still wallowed in pain. "Boys like you shouldn't play with guns," he said as he grabbed the ammunition belt from around the wounded man's waist. "Some-one might get hurt." Diego gave Max a venomous look, but the pain in both feet prevented him from doing anything. Crouching down again, Max started back towards the hole.

Colonel Sanchez watched in amazement as Max and Ilana executed their escape. He had been told that this "Missionary Max" was highly trained, but he had never expected him to act with such audacity. True, he was disappointed that he had not been able to observe a human sacrifice, but the escape...now that was a work of art. Someone who could pull that off almost deserved to get away with it.

Almost, but not quite.

Of course the Yamani girl, the red-head, and the air-head had already escaped, but they were of little consequence. It was unacceptable, however, that Max should escape. Sanchez looked up to where his sniper was in position, on top of one of the stone houses. He nodded and the sniper squeezed the trigger.

Max was thrown to the flagstones, a searing pain in his right shoulder. He had been hit. Gripping the ammunition belt in his left hand hand he gathered his strength. He knew he would have only one chance. He looked up...about three yards separated him from the hole. Behind him he could hear the footsteps of the warriors as they approached.

With everything that was in him he gathered himself up and took a flying jump towards the opening of the passageway. Something burned along his side, and then he fell into the blackness.

At the edge of the crowd, Sanchez cursed.

CHAPTER 23

CONSTITUTIONAL CONUNDRUM

The black Cadillac pulled up into the Pastor Dave's driveway and stopped. The tall blond man stepped out of the passenger side, and his friend, a small man of medium build wearing a fedora, got out of the driver's side. They walked up to the door and knocked. A slight wisp of a woman with auburn hair answered. She looked every bit the harried young housewife, down to the apron spotted with pancake batter.

"Can I help you, gentlemen?" she asked with a bright smile.

"Yes, you can." It was the tall blond. "We're with the government, and we're looking for one Regina Sherman. We have reason to believe that she is here. Now if you don't mind..."

"The government?" Linda marveled, her eyes wide. "That sounds very important." Then her eyes narrowed. "Which branch?"

The question caught the men flatfooted.

"I asked, which branch." Suddenly the wisp of a woman in front of them did not seem so wispy. "There's the executive, the judicial, and the legislative branch." She counted out three fingers. "Which one do you represent?"

"Um...."

"Wrong answer. Please leave...now."

"Missy," It was the short man with the fedora. "I don't think you know who you're messin' with here." He stepped forward threateningly, but suddenly their attention was drawn away by the sound of a small engine. The turned around to see a four-wheeler pull up onto a nearby snow drift. The rider, a young man in his twenties, had a hunting rifle resting on the handlebars–casually pointed right at them.

Before they could react a restored Ford pickup pulled into the driveway. It's tail swung around and they saw that the driver was none other than the cranky old man they had talked to earlier, only this time he was carrying a 12-gauge.

And then they heard the ominous sound of stainless steel being pulled back and snapping into place. They both turned around and found themselves staring into the barrel of a .38 Smith and Wesson, in the very steady hands of the petite housewife. Their hands shot up.

"Hey now, we just..."

Once again the short man in the Fedora was interrupted, this time by the short blast of a siren as a blue-and-white pulled into the driveway. Two officers stepped out.

"Everything under control, Dad?" asked one of the officers.

"I think so," replied Millard, from his pickup. "These two gentlemen were just leaving."

The drop from the opening of the shaft to the bottom was roughly twenty feet. Max crashed onto the floor and lay still. In the passageway that extended from the shaft three women stared in horror. In the light that streamed from above they could see that he was bleeding profusely from his right shoulder.

Ilana was the first to act. She rushed out into the light, intent on dragging Max back. Tanawehe and a somewhat recovered Mary Sue followed close behind. When they went to move his arms Max groaned, and it was then that Ilana noticed the burn mark on his right side.

"Just go..." Max gasped. "I'll...follow..."

"There is no way in this universe we are leaving you here," said Ilana in a tone that let everybody know the matter was settled. "The warriors will be climbing down here any moment, and we need to get as far away as possible, as quickly as possible. Tanawehe says she knows the way, so all we need to do is get moving. Can you stand up at all?"

With incredible effort, and favoring his right side and shoulder, Max struggled to his feet. Ilana draped his left arm around her shoulders. "Let's go!" she said.

Tanawehe led off down the narrow stone passage, with Mary Sue right behind her, and Ilana and Max bringing up the rear. As they walked Ilana used the ammo belt to make a sling for Max's arm.

"When we can stop for a minute we'll look at those wounds," she said. "For now, we need to move." Max could only nod in agreement.

The darkness soon enveloped them as they pushed deeper and deeper into the tunnel. Soon they had to hold on to each other so they didn't lose one another in the darkness. Several times they made sharp left turns, each followed by a flight of stairs, the space between them growing as they continued.

As they walked, the shock began to diminish, and Max began to regain control of his faculties, even as the initial adrenaline wore off and gave way to the searing pain in his side and shoulder. Still, Max was able to push the pain aside long enough to get his bearings.

They had been descending gradually for some time, so he knew they must be going deeper and deeper into the bowels of the pyramid. Unexpectedly, they came to a right turn, and this not followed by a stairway. After continuing straight for several feet, they veered to the right, then the left, then the right.

"Ask her where we are," Max groaned.

"She says we're deep beneath the city of Icxi Xahn," Ilana translated. "Very few people know this tunnel exists, and the ones that do know are afraid of it. It is called the tunnel of the Tan, the god of thunder. And..." Here Ilana paused and spoke again to Tanawehe, then continued. "...and apparently she's taking us to meet him."

CHAPTER 24

MESSAGE IN THE SNOW

"Well, so much for finding anything here."

Regina Sherman and Pastor Dave were standing in front of the charred remains of what has once been the Sherman family vacation cabin near Saratoga Springs, New York. When they arrived the fire department had already left and the fire inspector was just wrapping up his work. The inspector had been understandably suspicious of Regina–the fire had "insurance fraud" written all over it. Pastor Dave was able to satisfy the man's queries as to Regina's whereabouts, and explain a little of why they were there without going into too much detail. That, and Regina's obvious distress at finding the cabin in ashes helped mollify the inspector, who left the scene with a promise to "keep in touch".

Now the two stood in front of the ashes, unsure of what to do next. Their hope of finding anything at the cabin was floating away with the smoke that lifted lazily through the trees and into the atmosphere.

Pastor Dave looked thoughtful. "Whoever built this cabin sure had a good eye for location."

Regina smiled. "That would be my husband, the Eagle Scout. He took a lot of pride in how he set this place up. For me, this was always a great place to get away from the big city. For him, this was a passion. He used to love coming here with Max, and the two of them would have all kinds of adventures in these woods." She paused for a moment, and then looked with great sadness at Pastor Dave. "That's why, when I lost my husband, I also lost my son."

David Wilson's pastoral heart went out to the woman beside him. Up until yesterday she had been the paragon of success, president and CEO of the world's largest pharmaceutical company, accustomed to getting her way, and achieving everything she set her mind to. And yet...all this time, behind the rock-like facade, was a woman whose heart ached for her dead husband and wayward son–both beyond her grasp.

And there, before his eyes, the veneer cracked yet again. A sob escaped Regina's lips, and she sank down onto the seat of the snowmobile and cried. Her body heaved with sobs for several minutes. Pastor Dave sat down beside her and put his arm around her shoulder. They stayed like that for a few minutes, until finally Regina looked up at him, her cheeks tear-stained.

"They can have it all," she said, her voice barely a whisper. "The business, the money, the houses, the cars...they can have it all. I just want my son back. That's all." There was a pause, and then, "Tell me, Pastor Dave, what happened to my son when he moved here?"

"What do you mean?"

"I mean...when I last saw Max, he was an angry young man. Angry at his father for dying, angry at me for trying to...trying to make him make something of himself, angry at the world for what must have seemed like a million injustices. When he went off to war, he said it was for patriotism, but I'm pretty sure he just wanted an excuse to take out his anger on somebody.

"Then he came home, and he was still angry. The things he saw while in the Army hardened him, made him remote. We had fought before, but our fights turned especially bitter.

"Then he came here, and the next time I saw him, he was different. He was at peace. Even though he was on a runway being threatened at gunpoint by a madman, there was no anger. Concern for the safety those with him, but no anger.

"So I ask you again: what happened to him?"

And so there on the snowmobile seat Pastor Dave told Regina Sherman about how he had decided to stay late at the church one cold winter evening, how Max had seen the light on in the church and come in to chat, how the two had struck up a friendship, and how he had introduced the young man to Jesus Christ. And as she listened to the young pastor's straightforward account, Regina realized that this was something far different from "getting religion". She was familiar with the TV evangelists, the religious hucksters who stood on Fifth Avenue in New York, and the large revival meetings at Madison Square Garden. But Pastor Dave was not selling anything, had no agenda, no card to fill out. As he talked about Christ she almost forgot that he was referring to someone who walked on this earth over 2000 years ago–so personal, so deep was the friendship. And Regina found herself wondering if she had ever had a relationship like that with anybody, living or dead.

There was a long silence as Regina pondered what the pastor had just told her. Rather than try to fill the silence with wasted words, Pastor Dave stood up and wandered around the scene. George Santana's men had been thorough in their work. On the trip to the cabin Regina had filled him in on who Santana was–indeed his name was not unfamiliar. Most Americans associated him with political action groups and high-flying–if often shady–investment deals. There was no doubt that a man of Santana's wealth would have the resources to hire a thoroughly professional job. Obviously, his excessive wealth was accompanied by a complete lack of scruples.

As he walked to what had been the left side of the cabin Dave's mind turned once again to the beauty of the location. It must have been a marvelous spot to get away. Secluded, peaceful, hidden among the pines–and certainly no shortage of places to hide something of value.

Something had been gnawing at him since before his conversation with Regina about her son's transformation, and now he returned to where she was sitting.

"How much of this," he swept his arm indicating the surrounding woodland, "belongs to you?"

"We own about 500 acres...basically those two hills. But why?"

"Think with me." Pastor Dave was starting to get excited. "Your husband had a conference with Santana, where he comes to grips with the kind of man he was dealing with. The documents weren't in the car with him, which means either they were stolen from the scene of the accident, or he didn't bring them."

"My money's on 'stolen,'" Regina interjected.

"That could very well be," Dave nodded. "But if that's the case, why would Santana go to all this effort? Listen, if your husband was anything like his son, he was no fool. He would have put those documents—or copies of them—somewhere. He would have put them in a secure place, a place where they could not be easily found or destroyed...but also a place where someone who knew him *could* access them when necessary. Someone who knew him really well...someone like..."

"Max." Regina finished the sentence. "Those two traipsed all over these woods. There must be a dozen hideouts, forts and tree houses back there. I never went there...the Jacuzzi was more my speed. But they would come back from their adventures, all out of breath, and tell me about what ingenious tree fort they had built that day." She smiled at the memories. "After they told me all about their doings, they would go to the kitchen, make some hot chocolate, then sit down get out a notebook, and make their plans for their next adventure. Afterward they would gather up the papers and put them in..." her words trailed off.

"Put them where?"

"The 'top secret place'" Regina's voice was a whisper. Here eyes were far away, in her mind she was in the car as her husband was driving back to New York after his meeting with George Santana.

It's a snowy night, the roads are treacherous, but his SUV is more than up to it. The highway curves gently among the foothills of the Adirondack mountain range.

Suddenly a car appears out of nowhere and veers in front of him. Instinctively he swerves to miss it, and the SUV leaves the road and careens down the steep embankment, bouncing, flipping over at least once, brutally battering its lone occupant. Finally it crashes into the rocks of a small riverbed.

With utmost effort Theo Sherman reaches a bloody hand into his pocket and then removes it. Opening his palm, he takes a long look at the pocket knife, identical to the one he had given his son. Then he closes his fingers tightly around it, and everything goes black.

"I always thought that he was trying to use the knife to cut his way out," Regina murmured. "But...but it was closed. What if he was trying to tell me something." She turned to Pastor Dave. "Of course! I can't believe I didn't think of this before. They used their knives to open their 'top secret place.'"

Pastor Dave was about to ask where the top secret place was, but Regina was already walking. Then he saw where she was going, and laughed out loud. He followed her as she gingerly picked her way through the ashes to the only structure left standing by the blazing inferno–the chimney.

CHAPTER 25

THE WRATH OF TAN

Colonel Sanchez stood at the top of the ancient pyramid. The archaeological and historical value of the edifice was of no consequence to him. Neither were the confused, alcohol-soaked masses mingling at the foot of the temple. He had an objective, and he would blow up Icxi Xahn and everyone in it if that was what it would take to achieve it.

His troops formed a loose perimeter around the platform and extending down the stone stairway. The noonday sun blazed down on them. The crowd, frustrated once again in their desire for blood, had grudgingly dispersed. Beside him Owanalehe dusted himself off, his gelatinous folds jiggling with the effort. His excess layers of padding seemed to have saved him from injury except for the most minor of bruises. Diego was still lying on the ground moaning, clutching his newly wounded foot. Sanchez looked at him with scorn.

"Stand up."

The wounded man looked up at him incredulously. "What? How...

Sanchez motioned to the two soldiers standing closest to Diego, and they reached down and hoisted him up by the arms. This elicited a cry of pain from Diego. He lifted his feet so they were not touching the ground, and there he remained, hanging pitifully from the shoulders of the two armed men.

"Ask him what he can tell me about the tunnel," Sanchez ordered, indicating Olanawehe. Diego complied, then translated the response.

"He says the people tell him it is the entrance to a sacred maze, that nobody has gone into for ages. It contains a dark magic that terrifies the people. They say that..."

"Not interested in the history lesson." Sanchez cut him off. "I just want to know where it leads."

"Nobody knows," came Owanalehe's response via Diego. "They say there are many paths..."

"The only path that interests me is the one taken by this Missionary Max and his girlfriends," Sanchez grunted. He squatted down and ran his finger along the edge of the opening. Holding it up to his eyes, he smiled with satisfaction. It was coated with fresh blood. "Following them will not be hard." He stood up. "Gentlemen, let's go!" he ordered, and his troops prepared to descend into the bowels of the pyramid.

"Wait!" It was Diego. "Missionary Max took my gun. What if he's waiting down there in ambush?"

Sanchez cocked his head to one side. "Hadn't thought about that. Should be fairly easy to find out, though..." He motioned with his head to the two men holding Diego, and they moved towards the hole.

"Hey wait, what are you doing? No...wait...stop... Aaaaaaaaaaaaaiiiiiiiiiii!" There was a thud as Diego hit the bottom. Sanchez waited.

"No shots," he said. "All clear, let's go!"

"It sure would be nice to have some sort of light." Mary Sue had accompanied Max, Ilana, and Tanawehe in relative silence up until that point. But now the darkness was folding in on her, the stale air of the tunnels was affecting her, and she needed to talk, even if just to convince herself that she still existed.

"Pocket...pant leg...right side." Max gasped. Ilana felt down his leg, opened the snap on the pocket, and retrieved a small Maglite. With a flick of the switch the tunnel was bathed in a soft glow. Tanawehe gasped in wonder. The little group looked around. Behind them the tunnel stretched on forever. Before them there seemed to be some sort of entrance, and beyond that appeared to be a widened area.

For the first time Ilana got a good look at Max's wounds. The right sleeve of his shirt was soaked in blood coming from his shoulder. There was a tear in his shirt along the side, but no blood.

Ilana spoke to Tanawehe. "He needs to rest, and we need to stop the bleeding in his shoulder." The erstwhile queen of Icxi Xahn motioned them towards the opening in front of them.

As they approached, they saw that what appeared to be an entrance way as actually a place where the stone walls of the tunnel had been forcibly pushed outward, leaving jagged edges of rock sticking inward. Past those rocks, the fugitives found themselves in the middle of a large room...but not a room that had been carefully planned or constructed. Rather, the chaotic distribution of rocks and earth suggested some sort of explosion.

"What happened here?" Mary Sue breathed.

Tanawehe had no way of understanding the American girl's question, but her words, translated by Ilana, answered it: "The wrath of Tan!"

Ilana found a large rock with a relatively smooth surface and led Max over to it. He sat down heavily, his breath coming in short gasps. Without a word Ilana and Tanawehe set to work on his wounds, their fingers working in tandem, calling on all the training of their common Yamani tradition. Mary Sue, having been born and raised in the most technologically advanced nation on the earth, watched helplessly to the side. Ilana saw her, read the frustration on her face, and handed her the flashlight.

"Here, hold this. It will help us a lot." Mary Sue said nothing, but seemed relieved to be able to contribute in some small way.

Gingerly the two women removed Max's shirt. Tearing away the part that was already soaked with blood, they ripped the rest into long strips. Tanawehe took a couple strips and disappeared into the darkness, returning shortly having soaked the strips in water. With these they painstakingly cleaned the wounds. Then they stuffed some more cloth from Max's shirt into the wounds and bound them up. During the whole process Max gritted his teeth as wave after wave of pain washed over him. Finally, after they finished with the cleaning and dressing, he turned his head to assess the damage.

There was a red mark on his side where the bullet grazed him. A couple centimeters more and the damage would have been much more severe. The other bullet had hit him squarely in the shoulder, and it was still there.

"It's only a temporary fix, until we can get to somewhere where we can fix it up right." Ilana explained.

The light began to shake, and all three looked up to see Mary Sue trembling.

"Are you ok?" Ilana asked.

"I'm fine..." replied the frightened young woman, the tremor in her voice betraying the fact that she was anything but fine. "Just... just make him better."

Using the remaining strips from his shirt the two women bandaged his shoulder. "This will stop the bleeding" Ilana whispered. "As soon as we get out of the tunnels and into the jungle we'll be able to fix you up right." Max nodded, and leaned back and closed his eyes. Once again Tanawehe padded away, and then returned- this with time her hands cupped before her-bearing cool water. Ilana tipped Max's head back, and the refreshing liquid poured down his throat. Tanawehe retraced her steps three more times, and with each swallow of water Max could feel his strength returning.

Suddenly Ilana tensed. She motioned for all to be silent. Behind them she could hear the faint sound of footsteps. Without a moments hesitation she readjusted Max's wounded arm in the ammo belt around his neck, then hoisted him up, his arm around her shoulder. Tanawehe somewhat gingerly took the flashlight from Mary Sue, and once again the little group set off through the tunnels.

CHAPTER 26

THANKS, UNCLE BILLY

"L ook for some sort of loose brick," Regina said. She and Pastor Dave were gingerly poking around near the stone chimney of the burned out remains of the Sherman family cabin. "I don't know exactly where it was, but I do know they used to pry it open with their matching pocket knives. It was always a big deal for them." She chuckled at the memory. "When we came out here my husband became an overgrown boy, and this hiding place was a big hairy secret between him and Max." As he ran his hands over the stone, Pastor Dave could imagine the scene. A freckle-faced, red-haired little version of the Max he knew, having great adventures with his enthusiastic father. No wonder the fatal car crash sent the boy into a tailspin.

After several minutes of searching both of them came up empty. Regina leaned up against the blackened stone structure. "Maybe I'm wrong," she sighed. "Maybe I'm just imagining all this. Perhaps the accident was just that, and there is no grand plot."

"I don't believe that for a minute." replied Pastor Dave. "Look at all this," he waved his hands, indicating the destroyed cabin. "Somebody is out to cover their tracks." He stepped around to the front of the chimney, and the stone under his foot, what would have been the hearthstone, moved ever so slightly. He bent down and wiped the ashes away. The stone was large...but...he pressed it with the palm of his hand, and felt it give slightly.

"Regina!" he called excitedly. "Give me a hand here!" Producing his own pocket knife he scraped the soot out from the cracks between the hearth-stone and the other, smaller stones at the chimney's base. He noticed that the space on the side of the stone towards the chimney was greater than on the other three sides–big enough for fingers.

Regina saw it too, and without a word the two placed their fingers in the crack and pulled. At first there was nothing. Then the stone began to give, and suddenly came up all at once. Underneath was what appeared to be a pile of rags. Pastor Dave reached down and pushed them to either side, revealing a mahogany box. Carefully he pulled it up and set it in front of Regina. The cover opened easily, and Regina caught her breath.

The box was filled with paper. As she sifted through them she was assaulted with more memories of her son's childhood. There were treasure maps, secret codes, plans for tree forts and trails. Wrapped in a rubber band were faded Polaroids showing Max and his father enjoying all kinds of different activities–fishing, hiking, camping, building forts.

Regina was tempted to stop and savor each one. But she was on a mission, so, carefully, she lifted all the papers out. There, taped to the bottom of the box, was an envelope with the name "Regina" written on it.

"That's my husband's handwriting," she whispered. Handing the stack of mementos to Pastor Dave, she unfastened the envelope from the box and, with trembling hands, opened it. Inside was a single key, and a note.

"What's it say?" asked Pastor Dave. She held it up for him to read.

Uncle Billy's Christmas Present

Missionary Max and his companions stood in the wide chamber and stared. Unlike the previous chamber, this one was obviously built to precise specifications. A high dome was supported by ornate pillars carved out of the native stone. Ancient stone gargoyles with a meso-american feel peered from every nook and cranny of the stone structure, their features all the more grotesque in the dim illumination provided by the flashlight.

But none of this was of any interest to the party. Their gazes were locked on the centerpiece of the room. A giant suit of armor–half-again as tall as Max–stood on a raised stone dais in the middle. It reminded Max of pictures he had seen of Teutonic knights. The bucket-like helmet with a horizontal slits for the eyes, broad metal chest, imposing limbs, and yet...it was certainly not medieval.

For one thing, the design was too smooth...too industrial. A real Teutonic knight from the days of yore would be holding an imposing broadsword. This one was holding nothing.

The main difference though, was on the chest of the "knight". Where a true German knight would have boldly painted the cross of the Jewish carpenter, this monstrosity displayed the broken cross of Adolf Hitler.

Tanawehe spoke in hushed tones. "It's Tan, the god of thunder." Ilana translated.

"No...it's not a god...it's the devil," Max replied. Max's mind went back to the tunnel, and the large, coffin-like box. *Now I know what was in that.*

Tanawehe stepped forward, and knelt before the metal giant, her arms outstretched. She began to mumble in a sing-song voice, repeating the same words over and over.

Max and Ilana approached the imposing figure. Max reached out and ran his left hand over the metal. It was obviously industrial grade...not hand-tempered as a true suit of armor would have been. Also, the seams of the metal plating were held together with very modern-looking rivets.

Max knocked on the metallic leg. There was a slight echo.

"What is it?" Ilana breathed.

"I can't say for sure," Max answered. "But if I had to guess, I would say it was some sort of...robot."

Max began to piece things together in his mind. Somehow, a German ship flounders off Cabrito during World War II, not far from Esmeralda Island. The crew discovers the tunnel in the face of the cliff and lugs their precious cargo up there. They are surprised and annihilated by warriors of the Shadow People. These natives believe the objects they find in the cave to be gods and remove them the most sacred (and hidden) place they can think of—the caves under the city. They probably had to remove whatever deity occupied this dais in favor of the metal giant. Unfortunately, among the items they carry back are live ordinance for the U-boat's armaments. An unlucky fall, a big explosion, and the tunnel gets a new room—the one they stopped in earlier to tend to Max's wounds. Of course the Shadow People would understand nothing of this, and would identify the explosion with Tan, their god of thunder.

What surprised Max as he examined the machine was the good shape it was in. Over seventy years in a damp, underground tunnel, and not a spot of rust could be seen anywhere. Indeed, it looked like it had come off the assembly line yesterday.

And what was a ship with this kind of cargo doing so far from the Fatherland? Max wondered. The answer came easily.

Santana!

The faint sound of footsteps echoing behind them jolted Max back to their current situation. Unfortunately, further examination would be impossible. They had to keep moving. And so move they did, deeper and deeper into the tunnels beneath the city of Icxi Xahn.

CHAPTER 27

GEORGIA ON MY MIND

"Who's Uncle Billy?" Pastor Dave wanted to know. Regina laughed.

"My husband's family was very proud of the fact that they are distantly related to General Sherman."

"You mean *the* General Sherman? As in William Tecumseh...'march to the sea' and all that?"

"That's the one," Regina affirmed. "It's a running family joke to call him 'Uncle Billy'. My husband was thrilled when Max was born a redhead, said it must have been Uncle Billy's genes." She looked at the note again. "What I don't get is the 'Christmas Present' thing."

"Do you know anybody in Savannah?"

"Georgia?"

"Right. In December of 1864 Sherman wired President Lincoln, offering him the recently captured city of Savannah, Georgia as a Christmas present."

"That would make sense," said Regina. "My husband was a big-time history buff."

"Did he ever have any business in Savannah?"

"We do...did business in every major city of the US...and yes, I remember a couple trips to Savannah shortly before he died."

"Let me see that key." Pastor Dave reached his hand out and Regina placed the key in his hand. He held it up, inspecting it. There was a number on the side. *173*.

"If I had to guess, I'd say that was to a safe deposit box at a bank. Problem is, we don't know which bank. I imagine there are a lot of banks in Savannah."

"But how many of them do you suppose were operational at the time of the Civil War?"

"Not quite so many..."

"Come on!" Pastor Dave started back towards the snowmobile. "We'll grab a bite to eat in town, then hit the public library."

James Rockwell sat at a little sidewalk café, outwardly the picture of calm as he smoked a cigarette and read a newspaper. He was impeccable in a three-piece suit, fedora, meticulously shined shoes, and matching black sunglasses. Nobody would have guessed that he had spent a restless night in a fleabag hotel.

Nor would anybody suspect that he was a bundle of nerves. He was at the agreed upon place were he was supposed to meet Raymond Sand...but there was no sign of the grizzled American. Two hours had passed since the appointed time, and Mr. Rockwell could only assume that something had happened to him. He had tried to reach Francesca via his sat phone, but to no avail. Regina had been inaccessible since yesterday.

His newspaper was more a prop than anything else. The cynically named *A Verdade* seldom contained information worth noting. It's main value at the moment lay in keeping his *gringo* face hidden from curious passers by. He was about to fold it up and move on–to where he had no idea–when an item on the police blotter caught his eye.

Three men were detained by the military police last night in connection with crimes against the state. Two were Brazilian nationals, who have been handed over to the consulate of that country. Another is a common criminal named Nixon Sales, known on the streets as Cascavel. The three appear to have been involved in a plot against the State.

Mr. Rockwell put the paper down and took a long drag on his cigarette. There was a flight leaving from the airport in about an hour, a flight he was supposed to be on. His contact had not shown up, and he was forced to fear the worst.

But, reading between the lines of the article gave him the tiniest ray of hope. Francesca's two bodyguards–for he was certain this was the identity of the two unnamed "Brazilian nationals"–might be winging their way to Brazil right now, for all he knew. But Cascavel was in jail...which meant that Mr. Rockwell knew exactly where to find him.

But getting to him in a highly-guarded federal prison, that could present a challenge. Rockwell reflected back on how the officers had muscled their way into the SPGI factory and effectively expelled him from his own office.

Intimidation, he thought. *Two can play that game.* And with that he stood up, picked up his briefcase, tucked the newspaper under his arm, and stepped out into the street. For what he had in mind he would need an effective disguise.

Diego lay in an inglorious heap at the bottom of the pit underneath the stone altar. The Lightning Trooper goons had strode over him, around him, *on* him in their hurry to pursue their quarry through the tunnels beneath Icxi Xahn. After laying there for almost an hour, he began to stir himself. Slowly, painfully, he crawled over to the wall where hand- and footholds had been carved into the stone face.

One handhold at a time, he began to pull himself up. His arms shook with the exertion, and his feet ached from the bullet wounds inflicted by Missionary Max as they dangled useless below him. Yet onward he climbed, determined to reach the top.

Above him, and unbeknownst to him, Owanalehe stood with a contingent of Yamani warriors. Fingering the Green Monkey around his neck, he barked orders to a group of them and they took off through the streets of the ancient city into the jungle. The remaining group he directed to tidying up the sacrifice area at the top of the pyramid.

The fat witch doctor recognized that, with the departure of the white queen, there was a vacuum of power in Icxi Xahn...a vacuum he was determined to fill. And his possession of the Green Monkey–so long a symbol of absolute power for the Yamani– would bring this to pass.

His ambitions did not stop with the ancient city. After he had been named undisputed ruler of Icxi Xahn, he would wage war on the other tribes, and bring them all under his control. Then he would turn on the white men, sending his warriors into their cities and towns and cutting them down like slender palms. He had always hated them, hated their intrusion into Yamani lands and Yamani ways. The fact that he was working with them now was simply a matter of expediency. They had provided him with the opportunity to make contact with the Shadow People–little did they know that it would cost them their lives.

Then he would reign supreme over the entire archipelago!

Grunting with the exertion, Diego was almost at the top. He was also running out of strength. He reached up and his hand felt the stone rim of the hole. He gripped it with his fingers and swung the other hand up.

It was at this point that three Yamani warriors, under the direction of the witch doctor, pushed the stone altar back into place.

"Yeooooooooooooooooooow!" The scream faded, then stopped abruptly as Diego hit the bottom.

Owanalehe heard the scream and ordered the warriors to remove the altar. Peering down, he could make out the pitiful form of his partner in crime far below. The white man known as Diego was annoying at times, but he could still be useful. He motioned to one of the warriors and bade him fetch a rope.

CHAPTER 28

LOST AND FOUND

Lieutenant Sanchez stood in front of the metal giant. For the moment his quarry was quite forgotten. While his men fanned out to form a perimeter around the room Sanchez stepped forward and ran his hand over the front of the monstrosity, his fingers tracing the form of the swastika emblazoned on the front.

Stepping back, he reached into a pouch at his side and produced a laminated sheet of paper. There was really no need to confer–there was no way there could be two such objects on this god-forsaken island–but he did so anyway out of habit. The towering metal...thing before him was indeed the one pictured in the black-and-white photo given him at the initial briefing for this mission–right down to the last rivet.

Replacing the photo, he put his radio to his mouth and clicked the call button.

"Sanchez to base. Prime objective has been located. Repeat: prime objective located. Fugitives still at large. Request backup and further instructions. Over."

George Santana's trillion-dollar enterprise hummed the world over with the latest in digital technology. Everything was computerized and hardwired to the information superhighway.

Or almost everything. A conspicuous exception was the New York office of George Santana himself. Atop a high rise in the center of Manhattan's financial district, its furnishings had remained basically unchanged since Santana had taken over the family business over half a century before. On top of his large mahogany desk four items could always be found: a pad of paper, a fountain pen, a rolodex, and a rotary phone. Off to one side there was a small desk on which rested an ancient–but very functional–typewriter. Gigantic metal filing cabinets, organized alphabetically, took up one of the walls.

While he required all his subordinates to be fully versed in the latest technology, Santana preferred to keep his own life free from its clutter. There was a degree of calculated paranoia in this habit. No online connection meant that his most sensitive documents could not be accessed by hackers. But mostly, it had to do with his mind. His father had taught him that his success or failure would depend on how clearly he thought, and George Santana took that message to heart, systematically removing all trappings that would impede his mental processes.

And think he did. He sat now at his desk, hands together, prayer-like, his eyes closed. Years of experience had taught him never to be unduly optimistic. There were always things that could go wrong. But with that caution carefully in mind, he couldn't help but be pleased with where things stood.

The world financial situation was well in hand. Years–no, generations of careful investments had put him in a position where he could trigger a financial panic by making just one phone call. He had even done a couple test runs in years past, with satisfying results.

But history had taught him that financial panics alone would not achieve his goals. It was true that in times of economic crisis many looked to those in power for solutions, becoming even more dependent in the process. One example was the American welfare system, brought to life during the Great Depression and going strong today, despite a fundamental insolvency. But while many responded this way to an economic downturn, others did not. Indeed, during the lean 1930s Americans as a rule became more frugal, more thrifty, and more individualistic. And none of these were desirable qualities as far as Santana's plans were concerned.

No, for him to fully take advantage of a financial crash, it had to be accompanied by political and social upheaval. It was only when the whole world appeared to be going up in flames that people would cast about desperately for some source of stability. And so, with this lesson of history firmly in place, Santana had spent the second half of the twentieth century in a methodical effort to foment said upheaval. His numerous investments included radical political parties (both extremes of the spectrum), "social advocacy groups" bent on destroying the fabric of society, college courses taught by ideologues who molded the worldview of successive generations, and entertainment that deep-fried the minds of an increasingly experience-oriented society.

Back in the sixties, not content with the pace of his efforts, Santana had begun financing the production and shipment of illicit drugs to the western nations, while at the same time sponsoring legislation that undermined law enforcement. That had been a risky endeavor, and had almost caused his undoing when, years later, while researching the possibility of a joint business venture, the then-CEO of Sherman Pharmaceutical Group International had stumbled onto evidence of his schemes.

And just when he thought he had that mess all cleaned up, the late-CEO's son appeared out of nowhere and blew up–literally– the drug shipment program set up by his own son on their native Cabrito. George Santana still scratched his head at the coincidence of it all. He had thought that secret had died with Sherman Sr...but then came the call from Regina and the insinuation that she knew everything...had the father somehow communicated with his wife and son before his untimely demise?

It was a risk Santana could not afford to take, so now, as the time was nearing for the final execution of his plan, he had decided to eliminate the risk altogether. Hostile takeover of SPGI, hunting down of Max, elimination of Regina herself, and the burning down of the cabin in the woods, just for good measure.

Of course there had been a couple hiccups...there always were. Regina Sherman was supposed to go home, where she would be found a couple days later by police, dead of "self inflicted" wounds. Her bee-line for Upstate only confirmed to Santana the need to burn down the cabin, removing all possible evidence of what had happened.

That his two goons—actually part of a special intelligence branch of the Lightning Force—had failed to apprehend Regina was a minor annoyance. They were already planning their next move.

More irritating was the fact that Emídio had yet to eliminate the son, although prospects for that looked good. Apparently Maxwell Sherman had a knack for survival. But no such knack could long withstand the concentrated efforts of the Lightning Force.

And, truth be told, the elimination of Regina and her meddlesome son were only secondary priorities, sideshows to the main event.

The phone rang and Santana extended a bony, liver-spotted hand to pick up the receiver. He listened to the voice on the other hand, grunted his approval, and then hung up the phone with an expression on his wizened face that passed for smug satisfaction.

Yet another piece of the puzzle is in place.

CHAPTER 29

TAKE YOUR MEDICINE

Max and his companions shielded their eyes as they emerged from the underground tunnel into the bright daylight. It had been some time since they had heard the footsteps of their pursuers.

Squinting, the little band took stock of their surroundings. The tunnel had brought them out on a stone ledge overlooking a sheer drop off. The stone cliff extended several meters above them as well. To their left, water cascaded into a crystal pool far below.

The red-haired queen motioned for them to follow, and slowly–painfully in Max's case–they wound their way down an almost nonexistent path. It took them about half an hour to reach the bottom. Ilana made Max comfortable and began to attend to his wounds again. Tanawehe said something to Ilana then disappeared into the forest.

"She's gone to find some medicinal plants," Ilana explained as she started a small campfire.

Mary Sue wandered aimlessly around the pool, finally propping herself up underneath a tree. Before long she was fast asleep. Max reflected that his girlfriend had seemed strangely subdued. She had said almost nothing since their narrow escape from the Yamani temple, and she had avoided making eye contact with him. What had happened to her in time that had ensued since his capture?

Just as he was about to ask Ilana about it, Tanawehe came back, her hands full of various specimens of jungle flora. Together she and Ilana set to work on Max's wounds.

The ugly gash in his side was, thankfully, just a burn. Using the crystalline water from the pool they cleaned it so it would not become infected. .

Then they turned their attention to Max's shoulder. Here the bullet was still lodged inside, about two inches from the skin surface.

With the dexterity of one who had attended victims of spears, arrows and knives, Ilana cleaned out the area around where the bullet had entered. Without being told, Tanawehe found a couple sticks, sharpened them, and sanitized them in the fire. Max knew that these were to extract the bullet, and that it would not be a pleasant experience. He decided on conversation as the only way to keep his mind off the pain.

"What can you find out about our new friend?" he asked Ilana, who was splashing water on his shoulder. "She is obviously not Yamani...at least she looks like no Yamani I've ever seen...yet here she is, queen of the Shadow People."

Ilana looked over at the red-head, who, content with her two improvised surgical instruments, had turned her attention to the plants. Ilana put the question to her in Yamani, and the girl gave a lengthy reply.

"She says she has been revered by the Shadow People for as long as she can remember. All her life she has been told that she was a gift from the thunder god Tan–that one night there was a flash of light, and she was found floating in the sea. Her word has been law here, until the arrival of the fat witch doctor with his monkey pendant."

"I still don't understand the power that pendant has over the Yamani."

"I remember hearing about the Green Monkey when I was a little girl, although everybody said it had been lost. It was the kind of thing mothers told their children to scare them into behaving. Legends say that it came with the first Yamani to these islands. Supposedly it represented the power of some ancient god, and whoever held it would have tremendous power."

"I don't remember Owanalehe having that pendant before."

"He didn't, and I'm really curious as to how he got it." Ilana turned and spoke to Tanawehe again. She shook her head emphatically.

"She says he didn't get it from the Shadow People. They knew about the Green Monkey, but it was lost to them as well."

"So he just showed up with it one day?" Max asked. Ilana relayed the question to Tanawehe.

"Apparently so...together with the one she calls 'the hairy-lipped one.'"

"That would be our friend, Diego."

"And speaking of pendants, ask her about the one around her neck." Ilana spoke to the girl again, and she reached down and pulled the pendant off, handing it to Ilana, speaking as she did so.

"She says she's had it all her life, but the first time she saw inside it was when you opened it for her in the dungeon."

With his left hand Max popped the pendant open again. The happy young couple stared out at him once more through the faded photograph.

"If I had to guess, I would say that these are Tanawehe's parents. Based on what she is telling us, it seems likely that there was some sort of plane or boat accident, and that somehow Tanawehe survived and was rescued by the Yamani." He held the picture up for Ilana to see.

"Oh my!" she gasped. "That woman...she looks just like her, right down to the last freckle!"

"It's pretty clear to me that there is a birth certificate somewhere in the US, or perhaps England, with this young lady's name on it."

"I wonder what that name is."

"The last name, I have no idea. But her first name..." here Max snapped the pendant shut and gave it back to Ilana. "...her first name is most certainly Amanda."

Just then Tanawehe approached Max holding a large leaf cupped in both hands. Sloshing around in the leaf was some sort of liquid concoction. The redhead spoke.

"She says that talking can wait, right now you should drink up." Ilana translated.

Max opened his lips, and a sticky-sweet liquid slid down his throat. It burned slightly as he swallowed. For a moment nothing happened. Then suddenly the jungle exploded in colors. The world began to spin, slowly at first, then faster and faster. Then everything went dark.

Slowly, painfully, Max became aware of his surroundings. He was still in the same alcove by the glimmering pool. The soothing sound of the waterfall could still be heard behind him. The lengthy shadows indicated that evening was approaching.

He could still feel a dull pain in his side and in his shoulder, but it was nowhere near as intense as it had been earlier. Whatever jungle remedies Ilana and Tanawehe had employed, they had worked wonders. He felt refreshed and energized. He started to get up, and sharp arrows shot through his shoulder again. A cool hand touched his bare shoulder.

"Not yet, tiger." Max turned his head to see Ilana looking at him, a playful expression on her face. "You're better, but let's not overdo it."

Max slowly worked his way up to a sitting position with his one good arm–the other was still in its sling–and looked around him. Mary Sue was awake, but had not moved from where she had been sleeping earlier. Tanawehe was nowhere to be seen.

"Where's our new friend?"

"She went to scout out the area. We figured that our best hope is to try to get off the island...somehow."

Max looked up at the high, jungle-covered ridges that surrounded center of the island like an emerald crown. "So we have to go up and over?"

"Not necessarily," Ilana replied. "Tanawehe says there is a pass that will take us through the ridge to an inlet on the north end of the island. Apparently it's a popular fishing spot among the Shadow People, and there might be canoes there that we can use to get back to Cabrito."

"I don't like the thought of going back by canoe. It's obvious now that Santana is mixed up in this, and he wouldn't hesitate to send a chopper and shoot us out of the water."

"Oh, and speaking of choppers, one passed over us twice while you were out."

"Did they see us?" Max was not a little alarmed at this news.

"I don't know. We tried to stay out of view. But whatever the case, we need to get out of here as soon as possible."

Max agreed, then motioned toward Mary Sue with his chin. "How's she holding up?"

"She keeps to herself. We got food for her, but she didn't want to eat at first. I tried to talk to her, but she wouldn't answer."

"What happened out there in the jungle?" Max wanted to know. Ilana bit her lip before responding.

"I'll let her tell you that," she replied after a moment's thought. "Right now, you need to save your strength."

Max was about to protest when suddenly Tanawehe was standing there. Her arrival had been so quiet that she had appeared to materialize out of thin air. She spoke in low, urgent tones to Ilana. As the two women conferred, Max noticed that both were carrying freshly cut spears. They had not been idle while he had been out. With his good arm he reached down and patted the weapon at his side. The cartridge belt was neatly folded beside him.

"She says we need to leave, right now." Ilana informed Max when Tanawehe had finished. "The jungle is infested with warriors, and they're headed this way. She says it is only a matter of time before they figure out where we are."

Max was instantly on his feet, all pain forgotten. The idea of another race through the jungle with a horde of angry savages slowly surrounding them was not at all appealing to him. "Mary Sue, let's go!" he called. The American girl made no move to get up. "Come on, Mary Sue, we've got to get out of here!"

"I'm not going."

"What?" Max was incredulous.

"I've been nothing but trouble on this trip. Everything bad that's happened, it's all my fault. Just go and leave me here to die."

Max slapped his hand to his head in frustration. His girlfriend had insisted on coming, against his wishes, and now, when he needed her to come, she was staying put. He opened his mouth to argue with her, but Tanawehe removed all need. She darted over to where Mary Sue was sitting, unceremoniously grabbed the recalcitrant girl by the shoulder, and yanked her to her feet.

"Hey!" Mary Sue yelled, but she was already being dragged, half walking, half running, behind the determined redhead. Max looked at Ilana, they both shrugged, and then followed their hostess.

Tanawehe led them back to the the cliff, but instead of climbing it, they turned right and followed the stone face. The rock wall continued west, then curved north. Max understood that they were walking along the inside edge of the volcanic crater that was Esmeralda Island. After about an hour of walking they came to what appeared to be an outcropping of trees. And here, for the first time, Max noticed that there was a little cut in the cliff, concealed by the trees and undergrowth. Looking up, he saw that it extended all the way up. Two ancient, moss-covered sculptures stood guard at the entrance to a narrow, rock-strewn canyon. There was no time to closely examine the stone statues, but to Max they appeared to represent some sort of serpent.

The canyon was so narrow that it was evident they would have to travel single file. Without hesitation Tanawehe plunged in, dragging the still-protesting Mary Sue behind her. Max followed, with Ilana close behind.

"What happens if the warriors follow us here?" Max wondered aloud. Ilana put the question to Tanawehe. In answer, Tanawehe turned and held up her arm in a curved position, like a snake ready to strike. She hissed loudly to complete the effect.

"I see," replied Max. "And how can we be sure the snakes won't get us?"

Tanawehe laughed at the question, and gave her answer to Ilana.

"She says we can't be sure, but she would rather take her chances with snakes than with the spears of the Shadow People."

"Good point," agreed Max. "Besides, if we're lucky we might not even see a..."

His sentence was cut off by a loud *whap* that came from his right. He turned to see an ugly looking viper squirming on the end of a spear. Tanawehe let go of Mary Sue long enough to retrieve her weapon.

"On second thought..."

Tanawehe returned to the front of the line, grabbed Mary Sue by the arm, and once again they began to pick their way through the canyon.

Suddenly another sound brought them all up short. It was the unmistakable whirr of helicopter rotors, growing louder and louder. Looking up they saw a black shadow pass overhead, and the sound of rotor blades dimmed into nothing.

Cabritan Army, Max mused. *Hope they didn't see us.*

CHAPTER 30

PSYCHOLOGICAL TORTURE

President Oswaldo Ferraz sat in his office at the *casa branca*, and stared out the large window into the courtyard below. From the walls surrounding the grassy area, ancient cannons pointed their yawning mouths to the sea. Once, those cannons had represented the power of the mighty Portuguese crown over its Cabritan colony. Now there was no more Portuguese crown–much less a mighty one–Cabrito was no longer a colony, and as instruments of war, the cannons themselves were completely obsolete.

The *casa branca* commanded a view of the port area of Santo Expedito, and Ferraz watched in horror as a horde of metal giants disgorged from several landing craft and spread out through the city. His army tried to offer resistance, but it was pitiful, to say the least. Besides their metal armor, these robots boasted large guns that belched flame and destruction. Smoke rose from all areas of the city. Over at the airport the Cabritan helicopters were trying to take off, but suddenly the sky darkened as thousands of flying suits of armor filled the sky. Their guns bloomed with fire, and the helicopters were incinerated.

Obsolete...like a certain presidente *I know,* Ferraz reflected bitterly.

He looked out to sea, where the silhouette of the *Lua Negra* could be seen. Emídio Santana was standing at the rail, observing the destruction and mayhem with glee. Ferraz turned his attention back to the city, and with horror observed an entire platoon of steel men clanking their way up Santo Expedito's main avenue, breaking down the iron gate of the *casa branca* as if it were made of twigs, tramping into the reception hall, up the staircase, straight to the mahogany door that led to the presidential office, and...

Knock, knock.

"NO! I'll cooperate! I'll do anything you say..." Ferraz blinked and looked up. He was sitting at his desk, the door to his office was open, and Borges, his personal assistant, was looking at him strangely.

"B...Borges," he squeaked, trying not too successfully to maintain his composure.

"*Senhor presidente,* you asked me to inform you the moment there was news from the helicopters you sent out."

"Ah yes." The president resumed an air of authority. "And?"

In answer, Borges stepped forward and laid a piece of paper on the desk. "They were successful in locating Missionary Max and his companions. Here are the coordinates showing where they were last seen, and the direction they are headed."

"Excellent work, Borges!" Ferraz beamed.

"*Obrigado, senhor.* Will there be anything else?"

"Yes, please have the presidential helicopter fueled and ready.

"And where shall I tell the pilot you are going?"

"The *Lua Negra.*"

"As you wish, *senhor presidente.*" Borges bowed and left, closing the door behind him.

Playing the hero was fun while it lasted, Ferraz told himself as he busied himself with preparations for his flight. *Saving the country from the Santanas, going down in history as the great liberator...but that was before the metal giants. Now, I just need to make sure I'm on the winning side.*

Cascavel's slumber was interrupted by the sound of loud, angry voices echoing down the hall to his cell.

"You will let me in this moment, or you will answer to the General Council." The voice spoke in Portuguese, but with a thick American accent.

"But sir, I have no orders..."

"The incompetence of your chain of command is not my problem. Representatives of the International Commission on the Humane Treatment of the Incarcerated are to be given access to all prisoners at any time. Everybody knows that. Or perhaps you are hiding something...some gross human rights violation that needs to be reported to the press..."

That did the trick. "Please follow me, *senhor.*"

Steps echoed in the darkness. Cascavel sat up against the stone wall. Before long two men passed: one a guard carrying a lantern, and the other a bearded, bushy-haired man who, in the dim light, looked very put out. They walked past, then, suddenly,

"Stop!" The bearded man turned around and pointed straight at Cascavel. "That man. Who is he and why is he incarcerated?"

"His name is Nixon, he goes by Cascavel and he is charged with crimes against the state," replied the guard.

"Crimes against the state," snorted the bearded man. "Likely story. From the looks of him, he couldn't commit a crime against a fruit stand. Open the cell."

"But *senhor...*"

"Open it!"

The nonplussed warden fumbled nervously with his keys, finally finding the right one and opening the creaking cell door. The bearded man stepped in.

"You!" he addressed Cascavel. "How are you being treated here?"

The prisoner shrugged. "Can't say as I can complain."

"You see?" exclaimed the warden, triumphantly. The bearded man whirled around at him. "Obviously he's too frightened to give an accurate answer. Please step back while I talk to the prisoner, and do me the favor of keeping your mouth shut."

Shocked at this outburst, the warden complied, and the bearded man turned once again to Cascavel.

"Are you out of your mind?" he hissed. "Do you want to rot in here for the rest of your life?" Then louder, "So tell me, Nixon, have you been treated poorly here?"

And suddenly Cascavel knew what was happening, and who was talking to him. He let out a loud wail. "Oh, *senhor* prison inspector, it's terrible!" he moaned. "The beatings, the torture, the starvation..."

"Starvation?" The warden was incredulous. "He's been here less than twenty-four hours..."

Once again the inspector pounced. "So you admit there have been beatings and torture?"

The hapless warden opened is mouth, but no sound came out.

"Tell him about the psychological torture," Cascavel said, accusingly.

"Yes, do tell," the bearded man gave the warden a withering stare.

"There's...no...." the warden wanted to be a thousand miles away.

Cascavel motioned to the bearded man, who bent down next to his face. Cascavel put his mouth to the man's ear.

"Menudo," he said in a whisper loud enough for the whole block to hear.

The bearded man recoiled in horror. "You don't mean..."

Cascavel nodded his head sadly. "It's constant. And they seem to take special pleasure in playing songs from the post-Ricky Martin period. Everybody knows they were the never same after Ricky left."

The bearded man shook his head at the warden. "How you call yourself a human being is beyond me. I am officially taking control of this prisoner. You will have a lot of explaining to do at the UN." He shook his head in disgust. "Menudo!"

"But you can't just take a prisoner out of jail!" the warden protested, albeit rather weakly.

"Watch me," James Rockwell said, his voice dripping disdain. And, grabbing Cascavel by the arm, he proceeded to march down the hall, through the foyer, and out the front door of Cabritan Federal Corrections Facility.

Once outside Mr. Rockwell dragged Cascavel down a series of side streets until they found themselves in Praia Seca, the seedy port district of the city. Into a flea-bag hotel, up a flight of stairs to a room with a dirty window facing the road below, and finally they were able to rest.

Rockwell sat on the bed and pulled off the fake beard and bushy wig. Cascavel flopped onto a chair. "That was amazing!"

The American businessman smiled. "I must admit, I enjoyed that, probably a little too much. The look on the warden's face when you talked about psychological torture was priceless." Then Rockwell became serious. "Now we have to get in touch with Mr. Sand." Cascavel bowed his head. "What is it?" Rockwell asked.

"When I was on the boat with Francesca, we heard Santana talking to his goons, and they told him they had killed *seu Raimundo*."

James Rockwell sat up on the bed. "Ray...dead? I have a hard time believing that." He thought for a moment, then grabbed the newspaper that was sitting on the nearby table. Flipping through the pages, he finally found what he was looking for. He spread the paper out on the table and pointed to an item on the low right-hand corner of the last page. Cascavel read out loud:

The wreckage of a yellow Volkswagen was found early this morning, in the Rio Rocha. It is believed the driver fell asleep at the wheel and drove off the high cliff above the river. The driver is presumed dead, although...

Cascavel stopped, looked at James Rockwell, then finished the sentence,

...although no body has been recovered.

"Still," said Cascavel, after he had absorbed that information, "I know that area. That cliff is very high. I don't believe anybody could survive a fall like that."

"Whatever the case," replied Rockwell, reaching for one of the towels on the rack, "we'd best make a trip to the crash site. If Ray is dead, it's because he was murdered, and if we have evidence of it, it could come in handy." He opened the door to the bathroom, then turned to look at Cascavel. "One more thing...Menudo? Seriously?"

"Can you think of a worse form of psychological torture than that?" Cascavel asked innocently.

James Rockwell reflected for a moment. "No...no I can't," he said finally, and closed the door.

CHAPTER 31

IN THE HEAT OF THE KNIGHT

Even though Commander Sanchez had been fully briefed as to the capabilities of the "walking tank", he could not help but be awed at what he was seeing. As a boy he had sat on the knee of his maternal grandfather, an ex-Nazi who had found it convenient to relocate to South America after the war, and been regaled with stories of the glory days of Hitler's Germany. Papa had always hinted darkly that, had the *Führer's* secret weapons been fully developed, the outcome of the war would have been far different. Sanchez had always thought his grandfather a little touched in the head...until now.

Opening the hatch in the back of the unit, he let his eyes run over the amazingly well-designed inner workings. He motioned to one of his men to help him up into the small compartment.

Small...but not uncomfortable, the Argentine thought as he eased his legs and feet into their stirrup-like compartments. Next he pulled the headpiece down over his face. The retro-fitted night-vision goggles gave him a clear view of the cavernous room. He swiveled his head to where the engineer stood.

"Superb work," he said into his mike. The engineer smiled up at him. Based on the schematics of Hiler's "Victory Knight", they had developed a night-vision camera and a comm link to attach to the existing framework. Of course, never in their wildest dreams had they thought they would find the prototype in such pristine condition. They had always assumed that there would be much work to do in restoring it to its original condition, and had brought the necessary equipment to do just that.

Tentatively, Sanchez raised his right arm. The right arm of the metal suit raised as well–fluidly, smoothly, as if it were an extension of his own body. With increasing confidence the commander tested each of his limbs, with the same astounding results. He took a few ginger steps forward, then, gaining more confidence, he jumped up and down. The metal giant responded perfectly to each of his movements. The Lightning Force troopers gathered around and cheered every movement

Now for a test of strength he thought. Scanning the underground chamber, he saw a large boulder...the same boulder a wounded Max had rested on earlier in the day. He tramped over to it and bent down to pick it up.

It was like lifting a rubber ball. Amazed, he brought one arm behind his back and let the boulder fly. It crashed into the rock wall and shattered.

"Careful, sir, or you will bring the whole cave down on top of us," admonished one of his men. Sanchez turned, stretched out a metallic hand, and lifted the man up by his collar, bringing him face to iron face.

"That would be a problem for you, but not for me," he said, his voice sounding robotic as it came out of the speakers. There was a pause, then a metallic chuckle, and all the men joined in the laugh, albeit nervously.

Returning his subordinate unceremoniously to the ground, Sanchez continued testing the various movements of the marvelous contraption. It soon became evident that further tests would require him to leave the tunnel.

But first, they must tell Dr. Santana the good news.

Owanalehe stood at the top of the pyramid as the shadows lengthened over Esmeralda Island, and listened to the warriors' report with disgust. They had found the trail of the white missionary and his companions, only to give up the chase when the fugitives had entered the Snake Pass.

"Where will the Snake Pass bring them?" he asked.

"It doesn't matter," said one of the guards, shaking his head. "They will not survive. The serpent gods will not allow them to live."

The fat witch-doctor's eyes narrowed and he spoke through clenched teeth. "And if," he struggled to control his voice, "...if the serpent gods somehow fail to execute justice, where will they end up?"

The *onça* skin-clad warriors looked at one another, and their the leader spoke. "They will end up at the great fishing area, at the north end of the island, O Great One."

Olanawehe pursed his lips and eyed the commander. *This has to be the most useless man on the island*, he thought. Then he looked over at Diego, sitting on the steps, nursing his wounded feet. *The second-most useless,* he corrected himself. He turned back to the warriors. "Listen to me very carefully. You will gather every available man, and every available canoe. You will row as fast as you can to the great fishing area, and there you will capture the white man and the three women, and bring them back here. We *will* have a sacrifice."

The warriors bowed, then scurried down the stone stairway to carry out witch doctor's orders. After all, he was wearing the Green Monkey.

CHAPTER 32

GUN CONTROL

Tanawehe, Max, Ilana, and Mary Sue stood at a curve in the canyon. Before them was a rock wall that rose several hundred feet into the air. The rock wall on either side was just as steep. The canyon curved to the left, and in that direction, according to Tanawehe, the rock walls opened into a large wooded inlet, where they would be able to fashion a floating vessel of some kind and make for Cabrito.

Their trek through the canyon had been punctuated by the occasional sighting of a snake. Either Tanawehe or Ilana would dispatch the offending reptile with their spears, and the little party would move on. As they had penetrated further into the canyon, the snake incidents had increased in frequency, and Max was certain he noticed a general increase in the size and ferocity of the snakes themselves.

Now, here where the narrow path turned to the left–and freedom–was an outcropping of small rocks. and in the gathering twilight the rocks appeared to move. The hissing sound emanating from the area made it clear that their way was blocked by hundreds–if not thousands–of vipers.

And, to his alarm, Max realized that the hissing was not just coming from in front of them, but also from behind them. Turning, he saw the path they had just walked covered with the evil-looking reptiles. They were coming out of openings in the canyon walls and slithering to the ground. Tanawehe and Ilana unlimbered their spears, and two vipers immediately met their makers.

But they were just two out of many, and there was no way that the two spears were going to be able to get them through the tangled mess of serpents.

Max remembered the firearm at his side. Unholstering it, he filled the chambers. It felt awkward in his left hand. Shooting left-handed had been part of his training, but it was never something he excelled at. Still, he took aim and fired. The bullet thudded harmlessly into the canyon wall.

With great effort he tried to get his right arm out of his sling, but found that it was too weak even to hold the weapon. Reluctantly he handed the gun to Ilana.

"You try," he said. But though she was very adept with any number of jungle weapons, the revolver was unfamiliar in her hands. Awkwardly she gripped it and let off two rounds. Neither of them had any effect. The hissing only seemed to grow louder, and the circle where the four companions stood continued to get smaller.

Shakily, Ilana raised the weapon to take another shot, then she felt hand on her shoulder.

"Give me the pistol." She was shocked to hear Mary Sue's voice, and she hesitated.

"Please...give it to me." The American girl's voice was low and insistent. Still, Ilana clutched the weapon, not certain she wanted to entrust it to someone who had proven so inept at every stage of their journey. Mary Sue spoke again, a sense of urgency in her voice.

"You have to trust me," Mary Sue pleaded.

At that Iana's head snapped back. "Why should I trust you?" she hissed, angrily. "When I tried to help you escape back in the jungle, you turned me over to the enemy. How do I know you won't take that gun and shoot us all?"

Mary Sue bowed her head, and took a deep breath. "If it helps you believe me, I'll tell the truth right now." She looked from Ilana to Max and back to Ilana again. "You two are in love." Ilana looked at Max and found his expression to be just as shocked as her own. Mary Sue continued. "Don't try to deny it, you both know it's true. I knew it from the first time I saw you at the airport." Ilana was about to speak, but Mary Sue pressed her finger to the Yamani girl's lips. "That's one of the reasons I've been so horrid these two weeks. I realized that you two are made for each other."

"But..." Iana was searching for words, without success.

"It's okay. Back at the lagoon, while you two were patching up Max's wounds, I did a lot of soul-searching, and I came to the conclusion that I've been living a lie up to this point, and that..."

"*Hala nagana wahanaki!!!*" Everyone looked at Tanawehe, who was gesticulating wildly at the advancing snakes. There was no doubt that her words meant "The snakes are getting closer".

Mary Sue turned back to Ilana and held out her hand. "So to summarize: I've been a jerk, you an Max are in love and will have a beautiful future together...*but only if you give me that pistol.*"

Ilana looked at Max still uncertain. Max nodded. Somewhat reluctantly, she handed the weapon to Mary Sue, who balanced it briefly in her hands, then popped the magazine out of the hand grip. She reached over and took the ammo belt from around Max's shoulder, then thumbed bullets into the the magazine and clicked it back into place. Ilana was surprised at the cool precision with which her fingers worked.

"I'm next to useless in the jungle," Mary Sue admitted as she sighted down the barrel. "I realize that, and I'm very sorry for all the trouble I've caused. But there's one thing I can do. Ever since I was a little girl my daddy has been taking me to shooting ranges. Max even went with me a couple times, and though Mr. Special Forces here hates to admit it, I schooled him. A lot."

Under normal circumstances Max would have argued, but as these were far from normal circumstances, he decided to let it slide.

Mary Sue squeezed off three quick shots. Three serpents wriggled, headless, in the rocks. Another snake raised itself up on a rock close by, a shot rang out, and it's head disintegrated into nothing.

Max, Ilana, and Tanawehe stood in awe as Mary Sue casually dispatched eight more snakes before pausing to reload. Then she lifted the pistol again with both hands, her legs apart in a shooters stance. In quick succession twelve more snakes ceased to exist. She raised the barrel to her lips, blew on it, then winked at her companions before reloading.

Now she's just showing off, thought Max. She had pulled the same trick on numerous occasions after out-shooting him at the range.

Once again the revolver belched flame, and Max, Ilana and Tanawehe noticed that Mary Sue's shots were beginning to form a path through the squirming vipers. As she fired her next round she began to edge forward.

As impressive as Mary Sue's shooting was, Max saw that it would still be a challenge for them to get through the snake-infested area to freedom.

"Ilana, you and Tanawehe stand on either side of Mary Sue, and as she walks forward shooting the snakes in front of us, you spear any that try to get at us from the sides."

"What about you?" asked Iana, after translating for Tanawehe.

Max picked up a large rock with his left hand. "Me, I'll get any that come up from behind," he grinned.

Ilana nodded and motioned to Tanawehe and the two took up positions on both sides of the American girl. And so in this way, shooting, stabbing, and crushing, the foursome moved slowly through the sea of serpents towards freedom.

The rotors of his helicopter had barely stopped rotating before *presidente* Oswaldo Ferraz had his feet on the deck of the *Lua Negra*. With long strides he walked across the deck to the main cabin, and Santana's opulent office. For once he didn't mind being there. Bumping past a surprised Conchita, he flung the door open and stepped in.

The surprise on Santana's face at his dramatic entrance was pleasing to see, as was the surprise on the faces of the two officers of the Lightning Force.

"What is the meaning of this?" demanded Santana. Ferraz stopped in the middle of the room.

"*Doutor* Santana, Commander Krugel, Lieutenant LaRue," he gave a short bow in the direction of each as he mentioned their name. "I come bearing good news."

Santana leaned back in his chair and smiled that patronizing smile that usually drove Ferraz to distraction. This time, it didn't bother him in the least. "I don't know what your little piece of gossip is, but I'm sure it cannot compare in importance to the business that we are conducting here, so, if you will please..."

Ferraz didn't wait for him to finish, but placed the piece of paper on the mahogany desk.

"What's this?" Santana picked up the paper, examined it, then his eyes grew wide. "Are these...?"

The *presidente* beamed. The expression on Santana's face had made his evening. "That's right, *senhores*, while you were here on your little boat, conducting your 'important business', the Cabritan army has located your fugitives."

The two Lightning Force commanders shifted uncomfortably at the obvious dig. Santana rose from his chair. "*Senhor presidente* (Ferraz thought he detected a twinge of respect), it would seem that events are playing into our hands quite nicely." Here Santana gestured, and Ferraz, following his motion, realized for the first time that the huge TV was on. The image on the screen appeared to be an infra-red view of a jungle.

"You see, the little...toy...we were talking about earlier has been found, and it is in amazingly good shape. Our technicians have made a few minor adjustments, retrofitted some modern...er... conveniences, and we are preparing to run some tests. Isn't that right, Lieutenant Sanchez?"

"Roger that, *señor* Santana," came the reply, and it took Ferraz a moment to realize that the voice had come from the TV screen.

"By conveniences, *Herr* Santana means, of course, night-vision equipment, video cameras, a GPS guidance system, and an audio-video uplink." Commander Krugel offered, helpfully.

"Indeed," added La Rue. "*Eet* is all very...end of *ze* line, as *ze* English say."

"And now, we have the perfect test subject." Santana held up the paper. "Sit down, Ferraz, this is about to get entertaining."

CHAPTER 33

END OF THE LINE

James Rockwell and Cascavel stood at the bottom of the ravine, looking in dismay at what had once been Raymond Sand's yellow Volkswagen. The beams from their flashlights played over the wreckage. Cascavel shook his head, and wiped away a tear that was making its way slowly down his cheek.

Rockwell splashed around in the shallow stream, lifting up pieces of wreckage. "Look at this," he called to Cascavel. He held a piece of fender up for the other man to see. "Is that what I think it is?"

Cascavel examined the piece closely. "Looks like a bullet hole."

"That's what I thought," James Rockwell concurred. "And look here, there's more. A lot more." Cascavel looked to where the American was pointing the beam of his flashlight. Sure enough, just below the shallow surface of the water, what was once the rear hood of the vehicle...the part the covered the engine...and it was absolutely riddled with holes.

"Bonnie and Clyde had it good," Rockwell muttered.

"Bonnie and who?

"Never mind. And yet..."

"And yet what?" Cascavel asked.

"And yet, no body." Rockwell finished. "I wonder what could have happened to it."

"Um, *senhor* Rockwell, I think I may know." There was something about Cascavel's voice that made James look up, and he found himself staring at the business end of dozens of spears, held by wildly painted Yamani warriors.

Slowly, James raised his arms in the air. "Take me to your leader?" he offered weakly.

It was with a tremendous sense of relief that the small party of fugitives emerged from Snake Pass. The sun had set, and through the palm trees they could see the brilliant night sky. The cool sea breeze hit them like a refreshing wave, and they stood for a moment, savoring its feel.

Ever alert, Max began to analyze his surroundings. They were standing in front of an inlet, surrounded by gently swaying palms. A bright, full moon illuminated the ocean in front of them.

To the right of them was a large, dark mass that Max couldn't quite make out. He was about to go inspect it when the mass spoke to them, in English.

"It's been a fun ride, but I'm afraid it has come to an end." The voice was metallic, but there was a distinct South American accent. Two lights suddenly appeared like demonic eyes in the darkness, and Max realized with shock he was looking at the metal giant from the tunnel.

Tanawehe realized it too. She screamed in terror and shrank back, clinging to Ilana, who tried her best to control her own fear.

"You are surprised to see me here," Sanchez said as he took a step toward the little group. "This is truly a remarkable machine. My hat is off to the Germans and their engineering skills. Once we had this unit retrofitted I simply walked back out the tunnel the way we came in. It was entertaining to see the natives response to the giant metal monster as it emerged from their temple." Sanchez chuckled and took another step forward.

"The Cabritan Army kindly gave us your coordinates, and I set out over the trail that took us to Icxi Xahn in the first place. This suit makes it possible to run *very* fast. Once I reached the coast I followed the cliff, jumping over trees and and plowing through underbrush like it was nothing. I don't think I've ever had as much fun. Until now, that is." And with that he took another threatening step forward.

To Max's great surprise it was Mary Sue that reacted first. "Sanchez, you lying scum of the earth...." And before Max could stop her she had raised her pistol and emptied the clip at the metal monster. The bullets had as much effect on it as a mosquito would have on a battleship.

The voice came again through from the head. "Young lady, we *Argentinos* do not take kindly to insults from women. You will pay for that later. But for now, I'll be taking this..." And with that he reached out, wrenched the pistol from her hand and tossed it aside.

"Leave the women alone." Max stepped forward. "Get out of that tin can and come down here and fight like a man. Or are you a coward?"

"Coward, no. But smart enough not fall for that." And with a casual sweep of an iron arm Sanchez swept Max off his feet and sent him crashing into the undergrowth several feet away. Max lay there for a moment, the wind knocked out of him. The wound in his shoulder began to throb again.

CHAPTER 34

A GIANT PROBLEM

ack in on the *Lua Negra* the men sitting around the office were transfixed by what was happening on the screen. They were seeing the action from the same perspective Sanchez was, and it was exhilarating. Santana let out a whoop when the Argentine sent Max flying. "Get him again!" he yelled into the com link.

Obligingly, Sanchez turned his walking tank towards the prone Max. He raised his arm to deliver a devastating blow, but just as he brought it down Max rolled out of the way, and the metal arm crashed into the ground. The giant head swiveled, found its quarry, and struck out again. And again Max managed to barely avoid the blow.

"Get him!" Santana yelled at the screen, as if cheering on his favorite soccer team.

Max lay on his back, struggling to catch his breath. He knew instinctively that if things continued as they were, they were all doomed. Pain was shooting through his shoulder, and he felt his strength ebbing. Time was running out, and simply escaping the attacks of the giant would not be enough. He had to figure out a way to go on the offensive.

In the clear moonlight he spied the fallen trunk of a palm tree. Rolling over, he grabbed it and leapt to his feet. Mustering his strength he ran toward the approaching Sanchez, aiming the log like a pole vaulter.

*If I can trip him up and make him fall...*he thought, as he jammed the log between the giant's legs and twisted with all his strength.

But it was no use. The giant's legs were like Greek columns. Max felt the log wrenched out of his hand. The giant reached down, picked up the log, and broke it in two like a twig. One half he tossed behind him, while the other he held with both hands.

"You *americanos* like baseball, no?" Sanchez voice taunted him from within the bowels of the giant. "Batter up!"

Max staggered to one side, trying to avoid the log as it swung toward him, but he was too slow. The blow swept him off his feet, and again he crashed to the ground several yards away. He lay there, still, as the giant tramped towards him, intent on finishing him off.

Suddenly there was a metallic clang. Within the metal casing, the vibrations echoed inside Sanchez' head. He paused, then turned the head of the giant to see who had hit him from behind. The glowing eyes fixed on Ilana. The discarded half of the log was in her hand, and a defiant look was on her face.

"Come on, *covarde*, let's see if you can fight someone who's *not* wounded."

Sanchez was no fool, and he recognized Ilana's defiance for what it was: a desperate ploy to buy time for Missionary Max. She represented no immediate threat and, once Max was eliminated, he would be able to deal with her as he saw fit. He was about to turn back to the fallen American when he heard a voice in his earpiece.

"Kill her."

Back on the *Lua Negra*, Emídio Santana stood transfixed in front of the screen. President Ferraz and the officers of the Lightning Force were sitting around the room commenting approvingly on the conflict taking place miles away on Esmeralda Island, but suddenly Santana was oblivious to all of them. Before him, in the image projected on the screen...it was *her*, the beautiful yet ungrateful woman who had been foolish enough to reject him, and who had escaped his wrath that day on the runway.

Now here she was, like a small, helpless animal before the monstrous machine. Now, *now* she would pay for her defiance.

"Kill her," Santana said again into the com unit.

"But sir..." came back Sanchez voice. "First I need to..."

"KILL HER!" Santana fairly screamed at the screen. The other men in the room jumped. "That's an order!"

Lying on the ground, gasping for breath, Max watched the metal giant turn away from him and toward Ilana. He knew the island girl was buying time for him, and he also knew that if he didn't think of something, fast, she would be dead.

Gasping a prayer, he staggered weakly to his feet. As he took a step forward every bone and muscle in his body screamed in pain. Fighting back against the hurt, he forced himself to watch the giant. Ilana was scampering one way, and then the other, making herself as difficult a target as possible. Sanchez took a couple of swings at her, missing both times.

Desperately Max looked around him. To his right waves lapped peacefully agains the shore. In front of him, the raging metal beast drew ever closer to Ilana.

Water, metal...air...

It was a long shot, but it was all he had. With a plan in place his head cleared and the pain dulled into the background. He took another step, then another. His pace quickened to a fast walk, then to a run. As he did so he removed the tattered remains of his shirt, winding one end around his right hand. His brow furrowed and he concentrated on gathering up every last ounce of strength.

When he came within a yard from the back of the giant, Max leaped into the air. He gave off a grunt as his body collided with its upper torso. His flailing arms found the helmet, and he held on tight. At the sound of the impact, Sanchez stood momentarily still, affording Max the opportunity he needed. Desperately he found the free end of his shirt with his left hand and pulled the cloth up, covering the eye-holes.

"Guess who," he rasped.

Inside the bowels of the giant, everything had gone dark. Sanchez was completely blinded. He tried to reach up and grab the American from behind him. Max squirmed deftly out of the way, all the while maintaining his hold on the improvised blindfold.

Meanwhile, Iana had taken to beating the giant with the broken log. The blows were inconsequential, but the noise they caused inside the metal casing made it that much harder for Sanchez to concentrate.

"Sanchez, what's happening? Did you kill the girl?" Santana's voice in his ear didn't help him at all. The giant was staggering this way and that as Sanchez struggled to come to grips with this new situation.

I have to get this guy off my back, he thought, and proceeded to execute a series of movements designed to throw Max to the ground. He reached back with his arms, but Max managed to wiggle out of the way. He twisted and turned, trying to throw the tenacious American off, bucking-bronco syle, but to no avail. .

The moon shone brightly over the ocean, creating a scene as beautiful as the struggle was vicious. And it was on the ocean that Max pinned his hopes. He gave a quick, clockwise yank on the head of the giant. It responded by staggering to the right. Another yank, and another step to the right.

Inside, Sanchez was getting desperate. He put the hands to the metal face, trying blindly to grab at what was blocking his vision. But Max held on firm. Steadily the steel colossus moved towards the lapping waves.

Suddenly, just as the first metal foot splashed into the water, there was a sickening tearing noise, and the shirt in Max's hand ripped in two. Sanchez' vision was clear, but all he saw in front of him was water. He tried to execute a quick turn, but instead found himself falling headlong into the waves. There was a huge splash, and the giant lay still.

Ouside, Ilana and Mary Sue threw aside the log they had used to trip up the invincible "walking tank". Both of them scanned the water for some sign of Max. Tanawehe–who had wanted no part of confronting the thunder god for whom she was named–joined them.

The giant's fall had thrown Max further out into the waves. The girls spotted his still form floating in the distance. Ilana splashed into the water to where Max floated. "Max, talk to me! Oh please talk to me!" she moaned as she reached him and rolled him over. She could hardly contain her relief when he coughed up a pint of seawater.

Inside the giant, Sanchez' eyes flickered open. The impact of the fall had caused him to bump his head on the metal interior, momentarily knocking him out. He tried to move the arms of the giant, but found them unresponsive. The reason soon became apparent as he felt water creeping up over his body. Max's gamble had paid off. As Sanchez desperately unhooked himself from the mechanism he cursed the German engineers for not making their *Victory Knight* waterproof.

Ilana was helping Max to the shore when the metal door–still above the surface–began to rattle, then opened. Sanchez' head popped out, looking much like that of a drenched rat. He looked around him, trying to get his bearings, but froze as he felt cold steel pressed against his neck.

"You are the worst forest ranger I have ever seen." It was Mary Sue's voice. She stood in the water next to the half-submerged giant and held the recovered pistol to Sanchez' neck. Her grip was firm and unwavering, her finger pressed lightly against the trigger.

Sanchez craned his head around and looked at her with scorn. "You better put that down, little miss," he mocked. "You might hurt yourself."

Mary Sue's eyes narrowed. She looked beyond Sanchez to the shore. A small grove of palm trees grew about twenty yards away. "See that coconut?" she asked. Without waiting for an answer she raised the gun and fired. The coconut shattered. The pistol was firmly against Sanchez neck, as if it had never left. Sanchez' mouth was open in shock. "If I can't miss at that distance...well, you do the math."

"What are you going to do with me?" Sanchez wanted to know.

"I should put a bullet in your neck right now." Mary Sue responded. By this time Max and Ilana had splashed up to them. Tanawehe also arrived, adding the point of her spear to the pistol pointed at his neck. She let loose with a string of angry words. Max, swaying unsteadily beside the half submerged giant, was certain they were not very polite words, and a look at the blush on Ilana's face let him know he was right. He knew that if he didn't jump in, things could get very ugly, very quickly.

"Who are you, and why are you here?" he asked. "I have more than a passing knowledge of the world's armies, and I've never seen those before." He indicated the lightning patch on Sanchez' shoulder.

Sanchez was nothing if not professional, and at first he declined to answer. But when Mary Sue and Tanawehe pressed their weapons into the flesh of his neck, self-preservation took over.

"We are the Lightning Force, dedicated to serving the Santana family."

"I grew up on Cabrito, and never saw you before." Ilana observed.

"That's because we didn't want you to." Sanchez couldn't help sounding a little arrogant, even with a gun and a spear pointed at his neck. "Besides, our assignments are mostly elsewhere, depending on *señor* Santana's needs at the time."

"So why are you here now?" Max asked.

Sanchez indicated the submerged robot where he sat. "This, I suppose. The Santanas needed it for some reason or another. And they'll get it, too. They always get what they want."

"Except for this time," observed Ilana.

Sanchez laughed. "You've won a very hollow victory indeed, my friends. You have no idea of the kind of power you are up against." He was obviously warming to his subject. "In fact, if I were you, I would surrender to me, now. It might go better for you if I bring you in, willingly."

Mary Sue gave a snort and turned towards Max. That was all the time Sanchez needed. Sweeping his arms up he knocked the gun and spear aside and dove into the water. Mary Sue tried to follow his shadow under the waves, but it was too dark. Max put his hand on hers and signaled for Ilana to do the same with Tanawehe. Moments later they saw Sanchez emerge on the shore. He darted quickly for the opening in the rocks from whence the four had emerged a short time earlier, disappearing into the canyon. Moments later the small group heard ear-piercing screams, then silence.

The serpent gods had their sacrifice.

Emídio Santana's rage knew no bounds. President Ferraz and the two remaining officers of the Lightning Force stood nervously as he paced from one end of the office to the other, breathing threats and imprecations towards anybody and everybody that came to his mind.

"My weapon...my giant...they destroyed...that infernal American...that wretched Yamani girl..."

He stopped pacing and stood facing his three guests, panting heavily. Osvaldo Ferraz thought he looked rather like a rabid dog. There was even the slightest hint of foam at the corners of his mouth.

"I want them dead," he breathed. "I want them dead, all of them. I don't care who does it, or how it happens, but before the sun goes down tomorrow, they had better be dead."

There was a pregnant pause, then "Well? Why are you still here?" At this the *presidente* and the two officers fell over themselves to get out of the office and to their respective helicopters.

CHAPTER 35

THE OCEAN AIR

A s the sun rose over the Atlantic Mary Sue and Tanawehe stood at port and starboard of their makeshift craft and gently nudged it out onto the waves. Ilana sat towards the rear, cradling Missionary Max's feverish head in her lap. A short search after their fight with the metal giant had yielded two canoes left by the Shadow People who came to that part of the island often to fish. To the tops of these they lashed bamboo poles, forming a sort of pontoon raft on which they hoped to escape to Cabrito. The previous night's exertions had taken their toll, and Max was in very poor shape. The three women hoped against hope that they could make Cabrito before it was too late.

Twice Ilana had offered to take Mary Sue's place at the paddles, but the American girl would hear nothing of it. "Your place is with Max," she had insisted, and, truth be told, Ilana didn't argue that much.

They pushed off from the north end of the island and rowed east towards Cabrito. A sand bar stretched northward, and they paddled around it. Mary Sue was nowhere near as adept at rowing as was the read-haired jungle queen, but she stuck to her task with an admirable determination.

As they rounded the northern extremity of the sand bar, they could make out Cabrito in the distance, a lush green jewel rising out of the deep blue of the ocean.

But the eyes of the fugitives did not dwell long on this tantalizingly beautiful vista. Their attention was riveted on the horde of canoes in front of them, each containing *onça* skin-clad warriors, bows strung and spears drawn.

Regina Sherman stepped out of the First National Bank of Savannah and looked around her. The Georgia sun was warming the streets of the city. While it was obviously winter here, it was a sight warmer than Upstate New York.

Clutched in her arms was the package she had withdrawn from the safe-deposit box. Pastor Dave had offered to send someone from the church with her, but she preferred to do this alone. She didn't want to endanger anybody else with whatever information was waiting for her inside the package.

Now she wished she could have brought someone along. She felt very alone, and could never shake the thought that someone might be watching her. As casually as possible she placed the package into her tote-bag and struck off towards the hotel.

A few blocks and she was at the hotel. The smiling bellhop–the same one from the night before–was there. His name tag read "Rafael". He had fallen over himself to help her the previous night... quite literally. In fact, Regina had seldom met someone so clumsy. Still, she had given him a generous tip. Apparently this had made him twice as happy to serve, as he stood there waiting for her with that eager grin on his face. "Take your bag miss?"

Without waiting for an answer he took the bag and walked in front of her toward her room. On the way he tripped only once–a two-thirds improvement over the previous night–and fumbled for a couple minutes with the keys to her room. Regina stepped forward and opened the door herself. Red-faced, Rafael apologized profusely, handed her the bag, and turned to leave, sweeping a vase of an end-table in the process. Even as it hit the floor he was apologizing and promising to send someone to clean it up.

Regina closed the door behind him, then opened her bag to retrieve the package.

It was gone.

She opened the door to the hallway but Rafael was nowhere to be seen. Nor was he in the lobby. Nor did any of the receptionists or hotel management know of any bellhop named Rafael. And of course the security cameras were down that day...routine maintenance...so sorry...would you be interested in a week's vacation in any of our national chain of quality hotels, free of charge?

Regina went back to her room, flopped on her bed, and sobbed.

When she finally looked up, she noticed something on the bed stand that had not been there before. Closer inspection revealed a pocket knife—official Boy Scout issue—resting on a piece of paper. And it was not just any pocket knife. Crudely engraved on the side, in the handwriting of a twelve-year-old boy, was the name "Max".

Regina turned it around in her hands, a million questions forming in her mind. Then, out of the corner of her eye, she saw the piece of paper on the desk. Two words were scrawled hastily on it: "Sorry. Rafael."

As the canoes approached the raft, Tanawehe drew herself to her full height and let out a stream of orders in Yamani.

"She's commanding them to obey her, as their rightful queen, She's telling them how we defeated the thunder god, and how that shows how powerful we are." Ilana translated for Max, who had lifted himself up so he could see what was happening. One of the warriors shouted something back. "He says they serve the Green Monkey now," Ilana translated. Tanawehe scowled and muttered a few words under her breath. Max looked at Ilana, but she just turned slightly red and shook her head.

Mary Sue had the pistol in her hand, but everybody knew it would be next to useless against the mob in front of them. Snakes were one thing. Warriors with spears and arrows were quite another.

The canoes drew closer and closer to the raft, until the fugitives could see the details of the war paint on the Yamani faces. All of them bore some resemblance to the Green Monkey.

"Is the fat one here?" Max asked Ilana.

"I don't see him," she replied. "Oh wait, there he is." She pointed to a canoe in the lead. Owanalehe was in the front, and the poor warrior behind him was having a hard time reaching the water with his oar."

Just then the sound of propellers filled the air. Everyone looked up to see three "Hueys" bearing the markings of the Cabritan army hovering over the host of canoes.

"They don't look too friendly." Max observed.

The choppers nosed down, aiming their guns at the little boat. At the same time the Yamani warriors raised a war yell and drew back their bows and spears.

"Lord," Max breathed, "You've parted seas and rivers, calmed storms, and defeated armies." Cowered next to him, Ilana and Mary Sue offered their whispered prayers as well. Even Tanawehe, sensing that there was nothing else to be done, fell to her knees beside them. "To live is Christ, do die is gain," he continued. "But it's only gain for those who know Christ. We beg of you to show Yourself powerful on behalf of Tanawehe and all the Yamani here who know nothing of You!"

Max opened his eyes, and to his surprise he saw the helicopters turn tail and fly quickly away. *Probably content to let the Yamani do their dirty work*, he thought. Owanalehe's canoe was almost on top of them, and the fat witch doctor was standing in the front, a toothless grin spread across his florid face, the rower working overtime to keep the canoe upright.

"You lose, Missionary Max!" he shouted above the sound of the waves and warriors. His voice raised in a maniacal cackle.

And then his cackle was cut short as the water before them rose up in a white column, capsizing the canoe and sending its riders swimming for their lives. Other white columns erupted throughout the horde of canoes, and confusion reigned among the warriors of the Green Monkey. Dugouts went bottom-up and warriors struck out for the shore. The few canoes that avoided capsizing beat as hasty a retreat as was possible. Soon the ocean in front of them was as empty as could be, and the fugitives scratched their heads.

"Thank you, Lord," Max, Ilana, and Mary Sue breathed, almost in unison. Their brief praise service was interrupted by a loud blast from behind them that almost sent them headlong into the water. Turning, their eyes were greeted by the sight of a destroyer bearing down on them. At the prow they could make out Francesca Santana, flanked by her two bodyguards, Itamar and Inácio. From the prow blue and green colors fluttered majestically in the ocean breeze.

"The Brazilians," Max breathed, to no one in particular. "Remind me to buy some *bossa nova* CDs when I get home."

"That explains why the helicopters left in such a hurry," Ilana observed.

A lifeboat was lowered over the side, and soon Max and his friends were on the deck of the *Getúlio Vargas*. The precarious nature of Max's condition was obvious to see, and at the captain's orders the medics placed him on a stretcher bound straight for the sick-bay. Just before descending into the bowels of the ship, Max glanced toward the Emerald Island, and thought he saw a fat Yamani standing on the beach, fist raised in anger.

CHAPTER 36

THE END OF THE BEGINNING

Missionary Max stood at the rail of the Brazilian battleship *Getulio Vargas*. Beside him stood Mary Sue. Her shortened blond hair blew in the wind. Max actually found he liked the new style, despite the unorthodox way she had come about it–but he knew better than to express that opinion.

"So you're really going back to Cabrito?" Mary Sue turned to look at him with her big blue eyes. Max nodded his reply, indicating the raft that was being made ready at that moment to carry himself and Ilana back to the island. Mary Sue sighed. "Of course you are, and I wouldn't have it any other way. This is where God wants you, and so this is where you should be."

The two days on the *Getúlio* had been a welcome respite from the nonstop action of the previous week. While still sporting bandages on his arm and at his side, Max had responded well to treatment, and now he felt almost one hundred percent.

Mary Sue had been able to talk to her family in Greensborough via a telephone hookup, then she and Ilana had used the ship's

Internet connection to find out what they could about Tanawehe. Their search yielded information about the crash that killed her parents.

Tanawehe, however, was not around to hear the news. Shortly after their rescue she dove back into the ocean and struck out for Esmeralda. Ilana informed them that she had felt it her duty to try to save her people from the Owanalehe's grasp, and that now was the time to do it following his defeat. The others were sorry to see her go, and prayed that their paths would cross again soon. Mary Sue said she would take it upon herself to look up any living relatives that might be alive in the US.

As for the American girl, arrangements had been made for her to be picked up by a US Army helicopter and taken to Miami, from whence she would fly home to her family in Greensborough.

The one dark spot on the last two days was when Francesca informed them of Ray's death and Cascavel's imprisonment. Ilana had been grief-stricken, and she and Max had talked long into the night, sitting on the deck under a bright canopy of stars. With such a view, the eternal becomes just a little more fathomable, and Max spoke to her of Christ, of the cross, and of comfort. Eventually she closed her eyes, and her breathing became regular. He cradled her there for the rest of the night. And it was there, beneath the magnificent stars, with the moon reflecting on the waves, that Max knew without a shadow of a doubt that he would spend the rest of his life with this woman, and no other. As the boat gently rocked beneath him he whispered a prayer, asking God to give Ilana to him, and promising to love her and protect her honor from that point forward.

The decision to return to Cabrito was not a difficult one to make. Both Max and Ilana were aware of the risks. Yet Ilana needed answers to what happened to her father, and Max could not bear the thought of abandoning the Peace congregation. They decided to have the Brazilians leave them at a beachhead that was well into Yamani territory, close to the mouth of the Ipuna river and from there they would make contact with people in Santo Expedito. Even now Ilana was helping the sailors prepare the rubber raft that would take them ashore.

A Brazilian sailor called to them, and Max and Mary Sue walked over to where Ilana was waiting. Mary Sue gave her a big hug, then turned to Max. "She's special. Take good care of her, Max."

Max smiled at Ilana. "I intend to." Francesca appeared with her ubiquitous bodyguards.

"Cabrito is not exactly a safe place for me right now. I'm going back to my homeland for the time being. Are you sure you don't want to come to Brazil with me?" she asked. "There's a good deal of missionary work to be done there."

"And there's better coffee," offered Itamar.

"Right, better coffee," rejoined Inácio.

Max smiled, remembering his first encounter with this unlikely trio, back in a dark alley in Santo Expedito. "It's a tempting offer," he replied. "But my place..." he looked at Ilana, "...*our* place is on Cabrito."

"I figured you'd say that." Francesca smiled. "I'll be using my contacts in the Brazilian government to investigate the goings on here. Meanwhile, keep your heads down."

There were hugs all around, then Max and Ilana got into the rubber craft and were lowered to the waters. The Brazilian sailors rowed them to shore, helped them disembark, saluted, then rowed back to their ship. Max and Ilana watched it slowly move beyond the horizon, into the setting sun.

Max looked at her as she gazed out into the ocean. She was dressed in jeans and a white cotton blouse that Francesca had given her. Her raven-black hair blew in the wind. The simple beauty of that moment overhelmed Max's senses.

After several moments of silence, Ilana turned to him. "Well?" she asked.

Max was confused. "Well what?"

"Are you going to kiss me or not?"

She laughed when she saw his surprise. "You need to learn that just because someone closes their eyes, they are not necessarily asleep."

"You mean...back on the boat...you heard..."

"Every single word. I especially liked the 'love and protect my honor' part." She moved closer to him and looked up into his grey eyes with her smoldering black ones. "Maxwell Sherman," she said, laying on her sultriest Cabritan accent, "I know there are many things that will wait until our wedding day. But if you don't kiss me right now, there might never *be* a wedding day."

It was surprising how quickly Max recovered from his shock. He took her in his arms and kissed her, there on the beach, in front of the setting sun, with waves lapping gently on the shore, and gulls crying overhead. It was perfect.

And as the stood there in each others arms, five hundred warriors moved silently towards them under cover of the nearby jungle.

They were painted for war.

EPILOGUE

Two men stepped out to the curb at the Savannah/Hilton Head International Airport. One was a tall blond, and the other a shorter man with wearing a fedora. They hailed a taxi, and showed the driver directions to the hotel. The driver flashed a smile and pulled away from the curb. Through the mirror they could see his name-tag: Rafael.

It was almost midnight when an officer of the Georgia Highway Patrol answered an anonymous tip about an abandoned car. As he approached the vehicle–apparently a taxi–he saw two figures in the back. There was no driver.

The two men in the back seat appeared to be sleeping. The tall blond leaned up against the window, the short bald man lay with his head in the lap of his companion. The officer rapped on the glass but the two men didn't stir. He tried the door, and had to move quickly to keep the blond from falling out onto the ground as it opened.

After checking both men for a pulse, the police officer put in a call to the city morgue.

Just south of Jacksonville, Florida a black Corvette sped down I-95 towards Miami. In the driver's seat, Rafael whistled a cheerful tune and tugged on his new fedora.

...to be continued.

ABOUT THE AUTHOR

Andrew Comings is a Baptist missionary working in the state of Maranhão, Brazil. He is married to Itacyara, and they have two children, Michael and Nathanael. Their ministry includes church planting, theological training, and camp ministry. In his spare time Andrew writes, plays the saxophone, and dreams about having Brazil's largest model train set. You can learn more about their work—including the latest from the world of Missionary Max—at their website: andrewcomings.com

Other titles in this series:

Missionary Max and the Jungle Princess

MISSIONARY MAX AND THE JUNGLE PRINCESS

ABOUT THE ILLUSTRATOR

Zilson Costa is an artist and author from the Brazilian state of Maranhão. He graduated in fine arts from the Federal University of Maranhão and serves as a musician and art professor in local schools. His artwork has been featured in some of the premier comic book publishers of Brazil, and he has collaborated with well-known artists from Brazil and from the US.

Made in the USA
Middletown, DE
25 September 2016